A Kiss Before The End

A Kiss Before The End

Roy Glenn

www.urbanbooks.net

Urban Books, LLC
300 Farmingdale Road, N.Y.-Route 109
Farmingdale, NY 11735

ISBN 13: 978-1-64556-788-2
EBOOK ISBN: 978-1-64556-789-9

First Trade Paperback Printing March 2026
Printed in the United States of America

10 9 8 7 6 5 4 3 2 1

Distributed by Kensington Publishing Corp.
Submit Orders to:
Customer Service
400 Hahn Road
Westminster, MD 21157-4627
Phone: 1-800-733-3000
Fax: 1-800-659-2436

The authorized representative in the EU for product safety and compliance
Is eucomply OU, Parnu mnt 139b-14, Apt 123
Tallinn, Berlin 11317, hello@eucompliancepartner.com

A Kiss Before The End

Roy Glenn

Chapter One

One year ago . . .

Channel 4 news anchor Carmen Taylor heard that a friend of hers has died of sudden arrhythmic death syndrome, which is an unexpected death from cardiac arrest that occurs when the heart stops pumping blood, preventing breathing, and depriving the brain of oxygen. Carmen attended the funeral.

She had moved back to New York after she filed for divorce from her husband, Marcus Douglas. Although Carmen loved him, she wanted a divorce because he was never home. That, and she believed that he was having an affair with his law partner, Tiffanie Powers.

The straw that broke her back was one night when Carmen and Marcus had made plans to go out after she got off work. When she called him, Marcus was still at the office and had utterly forgotten that they had plans.

"I'm sorry, Carmen. I promise to be home as soon as possible."

Because of his commitment to his work, Carmen knew not to expect him anytime soon. She hung up the phone and looked around the studio.

This is my life now. A job I hate, and I have a husband that I love but never see, she thought.

Carmen was about to quit her job and call her lawyer, but she called Jada West instead and said that she was coming to visit her in Nassau. She and Carmen went to dinner at the Graycliff Restaurant, a five-star dining establishment that served continental cuisine with a Bahamian twist. Over John Watling's Single Barrel Rum, the two drinking buddies chatted about the circumstances that Carmen found herself in.

"You know, I hate to be in this position, but I did tell you that this was going to happen," Jada said.

Carmen laughed. "I know, and then you said, and when it does happen, don't come running to you, but here I am anyway." She paused. "I love Marcus with all my heart, but I'm bored with our marriage, and I hate my job."

"I think you should take a trip with me, perhaps go to Spain," Jada said, taking a sip of her cocktail.

"I like the sound of that." Carmen sat up a little straighter and leaned forward. "Where were you thinking about going?"

"I was thinking about us going to Barcelona, Spain."

"I'll drink to that," Jada said. Unfortunately, the trip to Spain did not materialize because after what was supposed to be a quick stop in New York, the murder of actor Mason Grant changed their well-laid plans, and Carmen immediately thrust herself into investigator mode. She called Ethan White, her producer at the station in Atlanta, and acted like she was reluctant to cover the biggest story of the year because she was on her way to Spain with Jada.

"I understand, Carmen. But if you do this for me, David has already authorized me to cover any charges incurred in rescheduling or cancellation, and he said you can take another two weeks off if you do this for me. What do you say?"

"Two more weeks, and if I want to come out from behind the anchor desk to cover a story, I have his blessing?"

Ethan agreed to Carmen's terms, and she covered the story. And then the offer came.

"I will pay you twice whatever they are paying you in Atlanta to come back to New York, Carmen. The anchor chair is yours if you want it." Which she did not. "And we'll give you the freedom and the resources to make *Carmen Taylor Reports* what you really want it to be."

"In-depth investigative journalism?"

"In-depth investigative journalism." Dan nodded in agreement. "I wanna make you the face of this station without putting you in the anchor chair. And once you and I define what that looks like, you will have the freedom and the resources to make it what you want it to be and what I need it to be."

Carmen accepted the offer, quit her job in Atlanta, and filed for a divorce from Marcus. When she returned to the city, Dan was as good as his word, and they defined what Carmen wanted the position to be. Since she did not like being in the studio, chained to the anchor desk all the time, and wanted to cover the stories that were important to her, Carmen would anchor the news from various locations depending on the story that she was investigating.

The funeral for Carmen's friend was to be held at The Abyssinian Baptist Church on West 138th Street in Harlem. That day, Carmen sat next to a woman named Victoria Howard. After staring at Carmen for a while, she could no longer contain her question.

"You're Carmen Taylor, aren't you?"

Carmen turned to the woman. "Yes, I am," she admitted.

Victoria held out her hand. "I'm Victoria Howard." She giggled softly. "I'm a big fan. So, it's such an honor to meet you."

"Good to meet you too, Victoria."

She looked around, and then Victoria leaned close to Carmen and whispered. “We know some of the same people.”

“Do we really? Who would that be?” Carmen asked eagerly; however, she was unprepared for the answer.

“Mike Black, Bobby Ray, and Carter Garrison.”

“Oh,” Carmen said in surprise. She looked around, and then Carmen leaned close to Victoria. “Do you mind if I ask how you know Mr. Black, Mr. Ray, and Mr. Garrison?”

She leaned closer. “I work for Carter Garrison. He’s my captain. I dance at Club Envy.”

“Oh,” Carmen said, and was a little put off. Carmen looked at the beautiful woman sitting next to her. “I hope you don’t mind me asking, but why are you dancing at Envy? With your looks and that body, you could be doing a lot more,” she said softly. Carmen leaned closer to Victoria. “How old are you?”

“I’m 21.”

“You could be doing a whole lot more with your life other than dancing,” Carmen said as the service began.

“Almighty God, we rejoice in your promise of love, joy, and peace. In your mercy, turn the darkness of death into the dawn of new life and the sorrow of parting into the joy of heaven; Amen.”

“We’ll talk later.” Carmen leaned close to Victoria. “Are you doing anything after the service?”

“Nothing. Why do you ask?” she inquired excitedly. Not only was Carmen Taylor talking to her, but now it also seemed that she wanted to get together after the service.

“Let’s go somewhere and have something to eat because I’m starving, and talk about it.”

“I would love to,” she replied enthusiastically.

Over a late lunch at The Bleu Room Restaurant & Lounge, Carmen talked to Victoria, who danced under the name Vixen, about a career in modeling over oxtail and jerk chicken. Carmen shared some of her experiences and how she had to change her life to get where she is now. She gave her the number of Calvin Clark, her old modeling agent. Then she called to see if he was free for an introduction. He told her that he was doing a show that night and told them to come to the presentation. After the show, Carmen introduced Victoria to Calvin.

"Nice to meet you, Mr. Clark."

"Don't talk. I just wanna see you walk," he said without so much as glancing in her direction, and he pointed to the stage.

Victoria nodded and stepped up and out onto the runway. While Calvin and Carmen looked on, Victoria walked.

"She walks like a stripper," Calvin commented.

Carmen giggled. "That's because it's what she does. She dances at Club Envy."

"And it shows."

Victoria stopped walking.

"I didn't tell you to stop," he said, motioning with his hand for her to keep walking. He leaned closer to Carmen, whispering, "She's beautiful. Absolutely gorgeous."

"I told you."

"Great legs. But that dress is too big, and it is totally wrong for her," he said of the white, high-low gown she was wearing. Calvin leaned closer to Carmen, but he kept his eyes on Victoria as she continued to walk. "It's your dress, isn't it?"

"Yes, it is."

"I thought so. But those shoes are hers, right?" Calvin asked about the leather lace-up wrap sandals that Victoria was wearing.

Carmen laughed aloud. "You've known me long enough to know I don't let people wear my shoes." Her body shook in disgust. "Repulsive."

"I know that's right."

"So, what do you think?"

Calvin was interested in Victoria. He thought that she had potential and agreed to train her and see where it goes from there. Over the next six months, she juggled working at the club and training for her first show. It was months of walking before he thought she was ready to wear designer clothes.

"The way you're walking right now is how I want you to walk the streets, and when you hit the runway, step it up a couple of notches."

"I understand."

Victoria worked hard, and she did well. Calvin kept working with her until he thought that she was ready to wear his clothes and appear in one of his fashion shows. She began doing more shows, and it started to conflict with her dancing at Club Envy. The fashion shows were usually on Friday and Saturday evenings. Therefore, Victoria arrived at the club late, and she got fined by dancer-turned-manager Vanessa Jennings.

"You need to decide about what's important to you and where you make your money."

"I don't get paid for these modeling shows."

"What?"

"I don't make any money modeling."

"Not making any money?" Vanessa frowned, shaking her head. "You need to get your priorities straight. Not making any money?" Vanessa pointed to the stage. "Go on and go to work. Not making any money," she repeated, shaking her head as she walked away from Vixen.

It was a month later when Calvin came to her with an opportunity to do a photo shoot with some other models in Nassau, Bahamas. Viven was excited about the opportunity, but it was on the weekend, and she would have to miss work.

Again.

But that was when she remembered what Carmen Taylor had said about having to change her life, and she agreed to do it.

Chapter Two

Nassau, Bahamas

It was a big day for Victoria. She was on her way to the airport to board a flight to The Bahamas. Victoria had never been out of the city before, much less out of the country. She didn't have a passport, so Calvin had to apply for an expedited passport so she could make the trip. It was also her first time on an airplane, so she was nervous about flying.

When they arrived at Lynden Pindling International Airport, Calvin and the models were picked up and taken in a van to the Courtyard Nassau Downtown at Junkanoo Beach. They had checked in, and four models were assigned a room. Once they were settled into their rooms, Calvin took them to eat dinner at The Bistro in the hotel.

"Get some rest tonight," Calvin rose to tell the models. "We have a seven o'clock call in the morning, and I don't want to see any of you dragging. That means no Señor Frogs, No Poop. And no Deck East, ladies. Are we clear, ladies?"

"Yes," the models said in unison.

However, despite that promise, thirty minutes later, Victoria and her roommates, Cynthia, Maya, and Candace, snuck out of their room and went to Aura, an adults-only nightclub in The Atlantis Casino. That night, Aura was featuring a DJ Competition with Nassau's hottest DJs.

"I'll see y'all later," Maya said when they arrived.

"Where are you going?" Victoria asked.

"To the casino," Maya replied as she walked away from her roommates.

"Go on with your bad self," Candace said. "I don't gamble."

"I can't afford to gamble," Cynthia cosigned, and the models went into the club.

"Neither can I," Vixen said.

For the next few hours, the three hit the dance floor. They danced with each other most of the time. Every now and then, a man would dance into their space, but after being ignored by the three beautiful women, they all eventually faded away.

As for Victoria, the professional dancer, she did a very conservative side-to-side two-step. Other than Calvin, none of the other models knew that she danced at Club Envy, and she planned to keep it that way. But when a song came on that she would dance to at the club, Victoria let her ass drop to the floor, and she came up shaking it.

"Look at you," Candace said to bring her back to reality, and she tried to giggle it off.

"I don't know what got into me," she said and went back to the side-to-side two-step.

It was just after three in the morning when the three decided that it was time to go.

"We need to find Maya and get back to the hotel," Cynthia stated as they left the club and went into the casino. For the next fifteen minutes, they wandered around the casino in search of Maya, but they didn't see her anywhere.

"Maybe she already went back to the hotel," Candace said and looked at Victoria, who was staring in the direction of the bar. "Do you see her?"

"No, but I do see somebody I know." Victoria discreetly pointed in his direction.

His name was Mitchell Wright. He worked as security at Shooters, another of Carter Garrison's strip clubs. Mitch was an extortionist, and he did a little loan sharking for The Family, but he was muscle.

The last thing I need is for him to say, "What's up, Vixen?" Victoria thought as she started walking in the opposite direction. However, it did cause her to wonder what he was doing there.

"Girl, he is fine," Cynthia commented. "What's his name?"

"Mitch," Victoria answered as two men approached him from either side.

"He doesn't look like he's happy to see them," Candace said as the men grabbed Mitch by either arm and walked him out of the bar.

"No, he doesn't," Victoria said as they kept looking for Maya until they finally found her at the blackjack table. Once she cashed in, they went back to the hotel.

They were all dragging at seven that following morning when the van came to take them to do the photo shoot at Junkanoo Beach. The shoot was to be broken into three parts. The swimsuits would be shot first thing that morning, casual wear in the afternoon, and the evening section would feature evening wear and gowns by up-and-coming fashion designer Chriscinda Parece. It was her first international show.

It was after eleven that evening when the van dropped off the models at their hotel. And after the long day, they were tired and complaining about their aching feet.

"I heard that some of you went out last night," Calvin began, speaking at the front of the van as they returned to the hotel. "Which explains why some of you were dragging first thing this morning," he said, looking at

Candace. "So, I urge you, ladies, get some rest. Rehearsal is on-site at eight o'clock sharp."

But that didn't stop them from sneaking out again. Their destination for the night was Cable Beach at the Rosewood Baha Mar Hotel. While Maya gambled in the casino, Victoria, Candace, and Cynthia went dancing at Bond at Baha Mar. It was after four in the morning when they returned to the hotel. The result was the same, and they were tired and dragging at rehearsal.

"I bet you all will get some rest now," Calvin said on the way back to the hotel. Since they were tired and dragging, the models got some rest that afternoon and were ready that evening when it came time to do the show.

The standing-room-only event was held at Utopia Gardens, which had a view of Corry Sound. Unbeknownst to Victoria, Mitchell Wright attended the presentation. The show was going well until Mitch noticed the two men who had approached him at the bar in Aura the night before.

How did they find me? Mitch asked himself. Knowing that he didn't have what they wanted, he began looking for a way out of there.

As the men got closer, Mitch rose to his feet. Maya had just come onto the runway wearing a floral, ruched, sleeveless midi-dress with Stuart Weitzman ankle-strap stiletto sandals. Mitch pulled out his gun, rushed up onto the runway, and grabbed Maya. She screamed as the two men pulled their weapons. Mitch fired a couple of shots at them and pushed Maya into the line of fire. When the men returned fire, Mitch ran. However, Maya took shots to her head and chest as she fell to the ground.

As chaos ensued at the fashion show, Mitch raced out of there, firing shots at the gunmen as he ran. Once the shooting stopped, the other models came out onto the runway as people rushed to Maya.

“What happened?” Victoria asked.
“Maya got shot.”
“Is she going to be all right?” Victoria inquired.
“I don’t know.”

Chapter Three

The return flight to New York was quiet the following morning. The group of models and support staff were all in their heads about what happened to Maya at the show. Chaos ensued following the shooting. The police were called, and the investigation into the shooting began. Although none of the models saw anything, they were questioned at length about the incident. Needless to say, the show did not continue when the police left; therefore, many of the models were disappointed on the flight back because they didn't get their moment under the lights on the runway.

It was no different for Victoria. However, in addition to sharing the feelings and disappointment that the other models were experiencing, she had the added burden of Mitch. When she peeked out to see how crowded the house was, Victoria saw Mitch in the audience.

What is he doing here?

Now, she was forced to wonder.

Is he involved in the shooting?

Did his presence on the island have anything to do with her or The Family?

Those were all great questions, but Victoria didn't have an answer to them. By the time the flight landed in New York, she had convinced herself that whatever Mitch was doing in Nassau had nothing to do with her.

If it were, he would have reached out and said something to me, right? Victoria thought.

On the cab from the airport, Victoria thought about whether she should mention Mitch being there to anyone. She had to work that night at Club Envy, so by the time she was ready to leave, Victoria had decided that it was in her best interests to mention it.

When she arrived at Club Envy, she went to the office to tell Vanessa Jennings, the club's manager, that she was back.

"How'd it go, Vixen?"

"The photo shoot was great," she said enthusiastically. "But there was a shooting at the fashion show, and one of the models got shot."

"Is she going to be all right?"

"She died on the way to the hospital."

"I'm sorry to hear that. But you're okay, right?"

"I'm fine."

"Good."

"I saw Mitch there . . ."

"Mitch?" Vanessa leaned forward. "What was he doing there?"

"I don't know."

"Did you ask him why he was there?"

"No, I didn't."

"Why not?"

"I never spoke to him. I saw him one night at a club we went to and again at the show."

"I see." Vanessa paused to think. "And you saw him at the fashion show?"

"Yes."

"Before or after the shooting?"

"Before. I didn't see him after the shooting."

"Was Mitch involved in the shooting?"

"I don't know. I was in the back getting ready when the shooting started, so I didn't see anything. I just thought it was strange or a weird coincidence that he was there."

The two women stared at each other in silence for what seemed like a long time.

"Go on and go to work, Vixen. I'll take care of this."

"Okay."

After Vixen left the office to get ready to dance, Vanessa sat there for a while, thinking about what she was going to do. She had known Mitch for years, but she didn't like him, nor did she trust him. She had been a member of The Family long enough to know that there was a family-run operation in The Bahamas. But Mitch was muscle, a leg breaker, so Vanessa doubted that he had any part of that business. She picked up her phone and made a call.

"What's up, Vanessa?" Carter Garrison answered. He was the captain of that crew.

"I need to talk to you."

"I'll be there as soon as I can," he said and ended the call. He glanced over at the woman who was in bed beside him.

"I know. You gotta go."

"Sorry," Carter said as he got out of bed.

"That's all right. It's getting late, and I need to get home."

Her name was Denita McKinney. She met Carter one night at J. R.'s when she was out with her girlfriends. She argued with her husband the night before, so when Carter whispered in her ear, the idea of grudge fucking came to mind. That was over a month ago, and Denita got out of bed thinking about how these interludes with Carter were saving her marriage.

"I'm going to jump in the shower," Carter said.

"Mind if I get in with you?"

"Not at all," he replied, and he scooped Denita off her feet and carried her to the shower.

When their eyes met, Carter's tongue attacked hers with fury, and Denita felt a river flowing between her thighs. His hands moved gently over her breasts. Carter squeezed them while he nibbled on her chin and sucked her neck. He eased her legs open and dipped his finger inside her. Denita closed her eyes and felt her body trembling. She bit her bottom lip to stop screaming. Carter caressed her thighs and then lifted her off her feet. She put her arms around his neck, and he thrust himself into her. Her eyes widened, her breath caught in her throat, her mouth was open, and her walls tightened around his length. Denita rocked her hips, clawed at his neck and back, then kissed and sucked his neck. Carter could swear he felt her juices overflow.

"Yes, Carter, yes!"

When Denita was dressed, Carter walked her to the door. Once she arranged to see him sometime the following week, Denita went home to see her husband. Carter walked back to his room, thinking about what he was going to wear. He had a reputation for always being impeccably dressed at all times. He opened the closet door, selected a Giorgio Armani two-piece suit, and laid it on the bed. He chose a Stefano Ricci silk satin tie and laid it on a black Saint Laurent satin overshirt. He nodded his head in satisfaction and began to get dressed. He completed the look with a pair of Ferragamo tassel loafers, and then, Carter left the condo.

Before he went to prison, Carter used to run a gambling spot for Howard Owens. He was Howard's top earner, but if you needed somebody to deliver pain, Carter was one of the best there was. Therefore, when Mike Black came to his spot, he said, "I need a good man to ride with me." Carter was his man.

"Where's Damian Pinkney?" Black asked Kyle Anthony calmly.

Carter reached back and punched him again, and this time, Anthony went down from the force of the blow. He stood over Anthony, kicked him in the face, and then stomped him repeatedly on his head, shoulders, and back. Then he grabbed Kyle and pulled him to his feet.

"Where's Damian Pinkney?" Black asked again.

But before he could answer, Carter reached back and hit him again, and then he picked up Anthony and threw him to the ground so hard that you could hear what sounded like bones cracking. Eventually, Anthony told Black that Pinkney had a meeting with Kareem Guy the next day.

"Thank you," Black said, and then he left with Carter. "Why don't you come get me tomorrow around noon, and we'll sit on Kareem until Pinkney shows up?"

"See you tomorrow."

The following day, Carter was lying in bed when the doorbell rang. He put on his pants, got his gun from under the pillow, and then he went to the door.

"Who is it?"

"Police."

Carter looked through the peephole and saw that it was two uniformed officers.

Fuck do these guys want?

Two hours later, he was still sitting alone in an interrogation room.

"We'd like to ask you some questions about Kyle Anthony," Detective Andrews stated.

As soon as Carter heard the words "Kyle Anthony," he knew there was only one word that was going to come out of his mouth.

"Lawyer."

Carter was arrested for assaulting Kyle Anthony. Anthony never mentioned that Mike Black was with Carter that night, and Carter never said a word. Carter was tried, found guilty, and sentenced to five years. He served his time at the Clinton Correctional Facility in Dannemora. As a reward for his silence and his loyalty, when Carter was released, Black made him captain of Howard Owen's crew.

When Carter arrived at Club Envy, he looked around for Vanessa. Not seeing her on the floor, he went to the office and knocked on the door.

"Come in."

When he entered the office, Vanessa was seated behind her desk.

"What's going on, Vanessa?"

"Same as yesterday. Making this money."

"How's it going tonight? I see the house is packed."

"It's been a good night. No problems, but it's early. I've been having a problem with some ballers trying to set up shop here."

"BBKs?"

"I don't know what these guys call themselves, but I'm handing it."

"If it becomes a problem, I wanna know about it."

"I'm trying to handle it before it becomes a problem," Vanessa said, and Carter nodded.

"What did you wanna talk about?"

"Mitch."

"What about him?"

"Any reason you know of for him to be in Nassau?"

"Nassau?" Carter questioned with his face contorted into a frown.

"I'm gonna take that as a no."

"Yeah, definitely a no. Ain't no reason for Mitch to be down there. Why do you ask?"

"Vixen saw him there this weekend."

"What was Vixen doing there?"

"She's been doing some modeling, and there was a fashion show in Nassau. And some shooting at the show."

"Was Mitch involved in the shooting?"

"She doesn't know. She didn't see the shooting."

"Is she here tonight?"

"She's out there on the floor somewhere." Vanessa stood up and went to the door.

Carter opened the door. "After you."

"Thank you."

Carter walked out of the office behind Vanessa, watching her wide hips swing as she went out onto the club floor. He remembered when she used to dance.

"I don't see her."

"I'll be at the bar," Carter said and walked that way.

As Vanessa went to find Vixen, Carter went to the bar. The bartender saw him coming and had a glass of Hennessy Paradis waiting for him.

"Thanks."

Carter took a sip of his drink, looked around the packed club, and thought about expansion.

"Hey, Carter," Vixen said when she walked up to him. "Vanessa said that you wanted to talk to me."

Carter turned and looked at the beautiful dancer. "Yeah. Let's talk in the office," he said and extended his hand toward the office. "Have a seat," he said when they entered the room. He sat at the desk, and she sat in one of the chairs in front of it.

"Vanessa said you've been doing some modeling."

"Yes," she said excitedly. "Carmen Taylor introduced me to her agent, and he's been working with me."

"Really? I didn't know that you knew Carmen."

"Yes. We met about a year ago. Like I said, she introduced me to Calvin. He was her agent when she was modeling. We did a fashion show this weekend in The Bahamas."

"Tell me about Mitch."

"Me and some of the other models were at a club, and I saw him there. Then I saw him the next day at the fashion show."

"Did you talk to him?"

"No. We were looking for somebody when I noticed him. He was with two other men, so no, I didn't talk to him."

"Tell me about the men he was with."

"We were getting ready to leave when I saw him. When the two men stepped toward him, they grabbed Mitch. I didn't see what they did with him after that."

"Okay. I'll look into it." Carter stood up. "Thank you, Vixen."

Chapter Four

After checking with Vanessa, Carter left Club Envy on his way to Shooters. As he drove away, he thought about calling Rain to tell her about Mitch. Since Black ordered them to work out whatever was going on between them, the lines of communication between Carter and Rain had gotten better. They were even able to work together, but it wasn't like it used to be.

And what if it were?

As hard as it was to admit, Rain had pussy whipped Carter, so yeah, if she were willing to open her legs, he would be more than willing to slam dick into her.

But that ain't happening.

And at this point, that was a good thing for Carter. If he wanted to be honest with himself, and these days, complete and total self-honesty was the order of the day, Carter would have to admit that the Rain Robinson experience had him fucked up for more than a minute. And it was an experience that he had no desire to live through again.

As it always does, it started out simple. They were just fuckin'. Rain Robinson was the best, most exciting sex that he had ever had. And then, one day, without explanation, Rain shut it all down. And then she fucked with his head.

Rain told him that she was pregnant with his baby, and she was thinking about having it. Carter had just begun not only accepting but also becoming comfortable with the idea of him and Rain as gangster parents when she told him that she had aborted the baby.

Since Carter occupied that other office at J. R.'s at times, Rain had begun hanging out at Purple and Deep Purple, the lounges that she owned, along with Mileena Hayes and Yarissa Dash. Carter avoided both of those spots because of his prior relationships with Mileena and Yarissa.

Carter and Mileena were in love.

Some would have said that Carter and Mileena were perfect for each other, and if you asked them, perhaps they would have agreed. But that was years ago. The love they shared was intense and passionate. But there was one problem that the intensity and passion of their love couldn't overcome.

For Carter, The Family always came first.

End of story.

And there was no room for discussion on the matter.

And that was never good for Mileena.

It was the reason that they had broken up before he went to prison. When Carter got out, he promised her that things would be different. They made a go of it for a while. However, once Black made him a captain and asked him to act as consigliere to Rain, who had recently been made boss of The Family, he reverted to his old ways. For Carter, that meant, once again, despite his promise, The Family came first, and, as you know, that was never good for Mileena, and they broke up for good this time. They had both moved on. Mileena was engaged to be married to a man with a successful dental practice, and Carter moved on to fuckin' as many women as he could to ease his pain.

Every man knows that's how you get over a broken heart.

Enter Rain Robinson.

It was just supposed to be sex, and that's all it actually was, but it still turned out badly for Carter. Although his heart wasn't broken, the Rain Robinson experience had him fucked up for a while, so the same remedy applied.

Fuck as many women as possible.

However, this time, Carter was sticking to the married ones. They knew what they wanted, and once they got it, they went home to their husbands. They got what they wanted and/or needed, and Carter protected his heart and his mind from future pain.

He considered it a win-win.

When he arrived at Shooters and went inside, it wasn't long before Don Horne, the club's manager, approached him.

"What's up, Don?"

Horne looked around Shooters and spread his arms wide. "It's all good here. What's up with you, Boss?"

"Let's talk in your office. I wanna ask you something," Carter said and started walking toward the office.

"Right behind you," Horne replied, following behind him. "Can I get you a drink?" he asked once they entered the office.

"Yeah," Carter said and sat down on the plush couch in Horne's office.

Horne poured them both a glass of Hennessy Paradis. He handed the drink to Carter and sat down.

"You heard anything about Mitch?" Carter asked and took a sip of his drink.

"Like what?"

"Somebody saw him somewhere where he didn't have any business being," Carter said.

Carter didn't think that Mitch was in Nassau on vacation. Black had told him about Jada's concerns about changes on the island, the most pressing of which was the increased presence and influence of an organization trafficking drugs on the island. Carter thought that if Mitch were in Nassau, it would have something to do with that.

"The nigga always has been kinda shady, but I ain't heard nothing."

"You heard anything about him and drugs?"

"Naw, like I said, the nigga is shady; but dealing . . ." Horne shook his head. "If he is, I ain't heard nothing about it. Why, what's up?"

Carter finished his drink and stood up. "Like I said, somebody saw Mitch where he didn't have any business being. I'm just trying to find out why he was there."

"While I got you here, there's something you can do for me."

"What's that?"

"Kelsey."

"Kelsey? Knuckles's wife?"

"Ain't no other, thank God."

Deserved or not, Kelsey Nelson's reputation around The Family was that she was a shit-starting bitch who shouldn't be trusted.

"What's she doing?"

"Hanging around here, pouching my top earners to work their gambling spot."

Carter chuckled. "It's a free country, Don. Women are free to apply their trade wherever they can make the most money."

Horne pointed at Carter. "You're right, they do. But fuck that shit, Carter. Bitch needs to stay the fuck outta my spot with that shit."

Carter held up his hands. "Calm down, man, I'm just fuckin' with you. You're right."

"Knuckles needs to stay out of my pocket."

"You're right. I'll talk to them about it." Carter's phone rang, and he answered. "Hello."

"This Rain. Where you at?"

"Shooters."

"Stay there. I'm coming for you."

"Okay," he said, and Rain ended the call.

As he left the office and went to the bar to wait, Carter was curious about what Rain wanted. When he got to the bar, the bartender poured him a drink and had it waiting for him.

"Thanks."

Carter took a sip of his drink and watched the women doing table dances. When he turned his attention to the main stage, Crimson and Sizzle were doing an exceptionally seductive and provocative dance that was tremendously enjoyable to watch.

"You ready?" Alwan asked when he walked up and stood beside Carter.

"Yeah." Carter shot the rest of his drink. "Let's go," he said and followed Alwan out of Shooters.

When they got outside, they walked to Rain's Lexus LS 500 F Sport. She was in the front seat waiting. Carter got into the backseat.

"'Sup?" Carter said.

"Let's go, Alwan," Rain said, and Alwan drove away from Shooters.

"Where are we going?" Carter asked.

"We're going to see Ibrahim Thomas, so you can make him tell me where I can find Lisa Përmeti."

"Who is that?"

"Nobody you need to be concerned with."

"Right."

Carter was getting tired of Rain's one- or two-word answers, but at least they were talking, and they were able to work together. He assumed the rest would come in time.

Rain sensed Carter's frustration with her, and knowing that she was the boss of The Family, she asked, "Anything I need to know about?"

"I don't know yet. Somebody said that they saw Mitch in Nassau."

"Nassau? What business Mitch got in Nassau?"

"None."

"What was he doing down there?"

"When I find out, I'll let you know," Carter said and sat quietly until they reached their destination.

Mona's was a relaxed Manhattan bar with distinctive brick walls that played live music. The spot also had a pool table and Skee-Ball. Alwan looked at the image of Thomas and spotted him at the pool table. He nudged Carter.

"There he is at the pool table," Alwan said, and they approached. He put his gun in Thomas's back.

"What the fuck?"

"Don't do anything stupid." Alwan took his gun. "Now, we're gonna walk out of here, nice and quiet. Understand?" Carter asked.

Thomas frantically nodded his head.

"Good."

Alwan pushed him toward the exit. "Walk," he ordered and escorted him out of the bar.

Once they reached the car, Alwan got out some plastic cuffs and a black cloth bag. He applied the cuffs, gagged him, and put the bag over Thomas's head before putting him in the backseat. Alwan drove them uptown to a house that Carter had never been to before. Alwan hit the garage door remote, and he drove in.

"Where are we?" Carter asked.

"Safe house," Rain said.

Alwan laughed and leaned closer to Carter. "More like her personal torture chamber," he said quietly as he and Carter escorted Thomas into the house.

Thomas was then taken into a room in the basement. The walls were made of concrete and lined with sound-absorbing fiberglass acoustic panels. There was plastic covering the floor and a chair that Rain had custom-made with arm and leg restraints and a hook in the ceiling.

"How you want him?" Rain asked.

"That depends." Carter took off his jacket and tie.

"On?" Alwan asked.

"I don't want you to fuck up his face," Rain said.

"Hook him," Carter said, rolling up his shelves, and Alwan hooked Thomas's cuffed hands.

Rain stepped up and pulled the black bag off his head.

"You're gonna tell me where I can find Lisa Përmeti," she said. "Or this is gonna be really fucked up for you."

Without waiting for an answer, Carter began punching Thomas in the arms, chest, and stomach until he had to stop to take a breath.

"Fuck you, bitch," Thomas shouted at Rain.

Carter punched him in the chest. "Watch your fuckin' language."

Thomas gritted his teeth.

"Tell me where Lisa Përmeti is, and all this stops," Rain said, and Carter hit him again.

"Fuck you."

"I'm tired of your shit."

Rain took out her gun and shot Thomas in the leg.

"Where's Lisa Përmeti?" she yelled, and then she shot him in the other leg.

"Shit!" Thomas screamed. "She's in Great Neck at a house on Arleigh Road."

"Thank you," Rain said, patting him on the cheek, and then she giggled. "You hang tight until we get back. If she's where you said she is, we'll be back, and you are free to go. But if you lied to me, we'll be back, and I promise, it will not go well for you. He's gonna beat you almost to death before I shoot you in the face. Understand?"

Thomas nodded. "I understand."

"Good boy," Rain said, once again patting Thomas on the cheek. "Let's go." Rain led Carter and Alwan out of the basement. "Go ahead and scream for help if you want. The walls are soundproof, so ain't nobody gonna hear you."

When they arrived in Great Neck at the house on Arleigh Road, where Thomas told them they could find Lisa Përmeti, Rain got out of the car and walked around to the trunk.

"So, what's the plan?" Carter asked, and Rain said nothing.

Without bothering to answer Carter or look in his direction, for that matter, Rain opened the trunk of her car and removed the M203 grenade launcher from her arsenal. She loaded it and fired. Alwan leaned close to Carter.

"Flash-bang with tear gas and iron bolts." Alwan shook his head and handed Carter a gas mask with night vision goggles as Rain fired again. "Very nasty."

"Let's go, Carter," Rain said, starting to run toward the house with Carter following behind her. "If anybody comes out, they're yours, Alwan."

As they got closer, two men came running out of the house, gasping for air. Rain shot one, and Carter blasted the other. Then they entered the house. Suddenly, two men appeared, firing shots at them. Rain turned in time to hit one of them with three shots to the chest before he could get another shot off. Carter shot the other and reloaded his weapon. They quickly moved through the house, firing shots and killing men as they moved deeper.

Next, three men came running at them. Rain shot one as he moved for cover. While the other two continued firing, Rain and Carter ran into a room and hit the floor. The two men blanketed the area with bullets. Rain and Carter stayed on the ground until the shooting stopped. Then Carter got up, moved quickly to the wall, and readied his weapon. Rain got to one knee in front of the door. When one of the shooters walked to the door and opened it, she fired and hit him with three shots before moving to cover. The other man ran into the room, and Carter fired and killed him.

"Ready?" she said to Carter.

"Let's go," he replied.

Rain came out the door, firing. Carter moved out behind her. He laid down cover fire while Rain ran up the stairs to the second level. Once she made it and was set, she covered while Carter ran up the stairs. They split up and moved through the house, looking for Lisa Përmeti.

Rain moved down the hall and looked into each room. A man came out of one of the rooms and fired once at Rain, but he missed. Rain raised her weapon and fired. The man took cover and shot back. Rain emptied the magazine and reached for her other gun. Finally, the man stood up, and Rain fired twice, hitting him with one to the chest and one to the head.

When two men came out of the room, Carter came up behind them and shot them both. He turned around and saw a man preparing to shoot. Carter dove to the floor as the man opened fire. Carter returned fire while lying on the floor. He jumped to his feet, and they exchanged fire. The man ran down the hall, and Carter shot him in the back as he ran.

Rain approached a room at the end of the hall and saw Lisa Përmeti coming out. She fired at Rain with an AK-47. Rain stopped, took cover, and fired back. When Carter arrived, he opened fire on Lisa Përmeti from the other direction. When Lisa returned Carter's fire, Rain stepped out and fired at her. She hit Lisa with three shots in the chest, and she fell to the floor.

Rain and Carter both stood over the body. Now, Rain shot her twice in the head.

"What was that about?" Carter asked as they exited the building.

"Nothing you need to be concerned with."

Chapter Five

"And that, Ladies and Gentlemen, is today's news. I'm Carmen Taylor, coming to you from Wall Street, where climate protesters from across the country converged to call on Wall Street to stop investing money in fossil fuels. Thank you for spending this part of your day with us. I will see you tomorrow at noon. Have a great rest of your evening. Good night."

"And we're out," the show's producer, Lacara Krisella, said. "Good job, Carmen. Great show, everybody."

After wrapping things up on location, Carmen returned to the studio to cut promos for the next day's news as well as her weekly news magazine, *Carmen Taylor Reports*. She was getting ready to head out when one of her assistants, Stephanie Zaire, who maintains her blog, stuck her head in the door.

"Got a minute?"

"I was just getting ready to leave," Carmen said and sat down at her desk. "What you got?"

"Do you remember the murder of Patsy McWalter about a year ago?"

"I sure do. It was one of the first stories I covered when I came back. What's up?"

Patsy McWalter was the daughter of Fredrick and Elizabeth McWalter. They were a wealthy, politically connected business couple. Her brutally beaten body was found in her apartment by her mother. The police have no suspects, and the case remains open.

"It may have been almost a year ago, but it is still an active conversation online. Well, you remember how Mom and Dad were playing Patsy like she was the reincarnation of the Virgin Mary, right?"

"Yes, I remember," an intrigued Carmen said.

"There's a woman who posted that she claims to know the real Patsy," Stephanie said, using air quotes. "Not the one her family is trying to make her out to be."

"If you think she's got something, bring her in. Let's hear what she has to say."

"I'll get right on it," Stephanie said excitedly.

Carmen stood up. "I'm outta here, Stephanie. Have a good night."

"Good night, Carmen."

"See you tomorrow," Carmen said, and she left the studio for the night.

Her destination for the evening was Knuckles's gambling spot. It was one of Carter's top-earning gambling spots, run by an enforcer and gambler, David "Knuckles" Nelson.

However, Carmen wasn't the only one going to Knuckles that night.

When Carter walked into the gambling spot, he was surprised to see somebody that he hadn't seen in years sitting at the bar.

"Carmen?"

Carmen turned to Carter and smiled. "Carter Garrison. How have you been?"

"I'm doing great." Carter scratched his beard. "Wondering what you're doing here."

"A friend of mine is dancing here tonight." Carmen smiled when she saw the look on his face. "Just dancing, from what she tells me."

"A friend of yours, huh? Who?"

"Vixen."

"Doesn't she usually dance at Club Envy?"

"She does. But she's doing a friend a favor, so she's covering her shift."

"I didn't know you knew her until recently."

"Yes. I've been working with her for a while now. Trying to get her work in the modeling business."

Carter nodded. "I heard she did a show in the islands. One of my men was there when the shooting started that weekend. You wouldn't know anything about it, would you?"

Carmen laughed. "Why would I know anything about a murder in Nassau?"

"Because you're a reporter." Carter paused. "That, and it happened in Jada West's backyard."

"Both of those are true. But I am not investigating that particular murder."

"If you hear anything, you *will* let me know, though, right?"

"I will, Carter." Carmen paused. "Especially since it happened in Jada's backyard."

"I appreciate you, Carmen," Carter said as Vixen came on stage to do her set.

Carter sat down at the table with Carmen and watched her dance for a while. Although he'd had a conversation with her about Mitch's murder, he hadn't really looked at her.

"She's very pretty." He looked at Carmen. "Kind of reminds me of you."

"Yeah, right." Carmen laughed. "Fifteen well-placed pounds and a lot of years ago, maybe. But yes, Victoria Howard is beautiful. Too pretty to be shaking her ass in here."

"I agree with you." He watched her dance for a while longer. "So, what's the problem with her modeling?"

"Her commitment." Carmen paused. "That's unfair. She has, let's call them, financial commitments, and those require money, so she has to work. And before you ask, yes, I have offered to sponsor her, but she turned me down. She said that feels like a handout, and she is very proud."

"I get that," Carter said as Knuckles came into the gambling spot. "I need to talk to Knuckles. But give me a day or two, and I'll see if I can work something out for her."

"Thank you, Carter. I appreciate that, and I'm sure Victoria will too." Carmen stood up and hugged Carter. "It was good seeing you, Carter."

"Good seeing you too, Carmen," he said and approached Knuckles.

"What's up, Carter?"

"Let's talk in your office."

"Sounds like I'm in the shit house."

"Nothing like that. We just need to talk."

"That's what I used to tell muthafuckas before I put two to the head," Knuckles said, laughing, and he followed Carter to the office. "Can I get you a drink?"

Carter sat down in a chair in front of Knuckles's desk. "Thanks."

He poured a couple of shots of Hennessy and handed one to Carter.

"What's up?"

"You heard anything about Mitch?"

"I know Mitch is into a lot of shit."

"Like?"

"I know he's got a robbing crew. They hit warehouses, steal cars, shit like that."

"Shit. I know that. Tell me something I don't know."

Knuckles shrugged his shoulders. "I haven't heard anything out of the way. Why?"

"Just asking."

"Bullshit, but okay."

"What's this I hear about Kelsey getting dancers from Shooters to work your spots?"

"It's her job to recruit the top talent."

"I get that. But why does she have to recruit Don's top talent?"

"Because Don has some of the top talent in the city, that's why."

"Is she recruiting from my other spots too?"

"Yeah."

Carter shook his head. "That stops tonight."

"Understood."

Carter finished his drink and stood up. "I'm out."

"You want me to ask some questions about what Mitch is up to?"

"Do that. Let me know if you hear anything interesting."

"Will do," Knuckles said, and Carter left his office.

An hour later, Kelsey arrived at the office. She fixed a drink for herself and another for Knuckles and came to sit down.

"What you hear about Mitch?"

"I hear he's got something going on. I know he's been flashing a lot of paper lately. He dropped a chunk of it here a couple of times. Why, what's up?"

"Find out what the nigga's into."

"Who wants to know?"

"I do."

"Okay." Kelsey finished her drink. "I'm going home. You gonna be here all night?"

"Probably. One more thing before you go."

"What's that?"

"Don complained to Carter about you recruiting his women to work here."

"What can I say? I just offer them an opportunity to make more money."

"Whatever, Kelsey. Carter's exact words were, 'It stops tonight.'"

"Whatever the Skipper wants, the Skipper gets. I'll just be more discreet. But I am not gonna stop recruiting the best pussy-slinging hustlers to work our spot," Kelsey said.

Chapter Six

Mercedes rose to power the night that three of Gee Cameron's men forced their way into the gambling house and killed Cynt. That night, Black left Treach in charge, and Rain told Mercedes to help him. Immediately after Black, Bobby, and Rain left Cynt's that night, Mercedes left the floor and quickly took off the outfit she was wearing. When she emerged, she was wearing a Donna Karan tuxedo jacket with stretch jersey wide-leg pants and headed straight for the gambling room.

Slater ran the gambling there, so Mercedes knew that she would need him with her.

"So you runnin' things now?" Slater asked when Mercedes came through the door.

"Until Rain says different," she said with authority.

The Mercedes takeover of Cynt's took less than two hours.

Mercedes thought about the night that she went into the office and was surprised to see somebody seated in one of the chairs in front of the desk.

"Who are you?"

"My name is Jada West."

Mercedes had heard about Jada West and was instantly suspicious.

"Okay. Now, what the fuck are you doing in here?"

Black, who was sitting in the chair behind the desk, spun around.

"She's talking to me."

He introduced Mercedes and Jada. After Jada left, Black explained why she was there.

"For more than just the obvious reasons, I've been watching you, Mercedes. I watched you become one of the top earners in here. And you did it without selling yourself. Then I watched you manipulate Cynt, which wasn't easy. Then you made yourself extremely useful to Nick. All to enhance your power. And I watched you purposely piss off Rain on a regular basis. Not enough for her to kill you, but just enough to impress her and let her know that you were the right one to sit in this chair." Black paused. "Here's what's gonna happen. I'm gonna separate the gambling from the dancers. You are going to take over the gambling in a new location. The reason I introduced you to Ms. West is that she's gonna recruit the ladies to work there and teach you how I want that house run."

Once Jada recruited the women, she returned to Paraíso in Nassau with Mercedes. By the time she took the women back to New York, Mercedes, who was initially resistant to Jada's methods, understood the difference between being the product and being the woman who is presenting the product.

When she returned to New York, Black opened La Chat and handed it to Mercedes. He intended it to be an upscale gambling spot that would rival Paraíso. And then Black met Veronica Rose.

Black, Rain, and his brother Elias were looking for a killer that they called Madman, and were told that he liked a singer who sang at Small's Jazz Club in Greenwich Village. Black was enjoying Veronica Rose and the band on stage jamming, and Rain was in Madman's boy, Jajuante's, face, starting shit when Madman came down the steps.

When the shooting started, Rain pulled her guns and dove to the floor, while Black dove over the bar as he fired. A lull in the shooting gave Black and Rain the time to get to their feet. Rain hit Quan with two shots to the chest. When he went down, Black aimed at and shot Jajuante. But Madman got away.

When the shooting stopped, Rain saw Veronica Rose get up from the stage. Rain rushed up on stage and grabbed her by the arm. She led Veronica through the exit door that opened into an alley. Black and Elias came out behind her and went to their car. Once they were in Rain's car, Black got in the backseat with Veronica.

"I just need to know where to find Madman," he said.

"I swear I don't know where to find him," a very scared Veronica said quickly. "That maniac and his goons just started showing up at places where I work. At first, I thought it was cute . . . until he started talking to me."

After that, Black asked her if they could drop her off somewhere, and Rain drove in that direction. On the way, Black told her how much he enjoyed listening to her sing.

"I have an associate who runs a very exclusive club for a very exclusive clientele. We've been talking about adding a jazz trio. I think you have the perfect voice for that establishment."

Black put Veronica in touch with Mercedes, and she's been appearing there nightly ever since. When people started coming there to hear Veronica Rose sing jazz standards, Mercedes saw an opportunity. She expanded the size of the show floor. Then Mercedes renovated her spot to include a kitchen, and she hired a chef.

Now that there was more than just gambling at La Chat, the clientele grew. La Chat was now the premium private club in the city—the finest food and entertainment, where admission was by reservation only.

On his way to La Chat, Carter called Geno and told him to meet him there. When he arrived, he looked around for Geno, but he did not see him, so Carter went and talked to Mercedes.

"Good evening, Mr. Garrison."

"Evening, Mercedes. How's it going?"

"We are having an excellent night."

Carter looked around at all the people standing at the bars and around the show floor. "Standing room only?" he questioned.

"Yes, sir."

"Any problems I need to know about?"

"Of course not," Mercedes said as if she were insulted by the question.

"You never do."

"Jada taught me to run a nice, quiet program, and that's what I do." Mercedes looked up on stage and raised one finger. "Well, I do have one problem."

"What's that?"

"I need a new house band."

Carter looked up on stage and then at Mercedes. "Who are those guys?"

"That's Veronica's band. The house band quit. They got an offer to headline for more money."

"I understand. I know you can handle it, but I'll make some inquiries and get back to you in a day or two."

"Thank you, Mr. Garrison."

"What can you tell me about Mitch?"

"Mitch Wright? That he's a grimy bastard that I had to ban from coming here."

"Why did you ban him from your spot?"

"Too many of my ladies requested it because of the way he treats them, and then he doesn't want to pay. He is a poor gambler, so he spent a great deal of money here, but he still had to go."

"You know any reason for him to be in Nassau?"

Mercedes paused to think. "Only one reason I can think of. Well, two, actually. He could be there on vacation. But somehow, Mitch doesn't impress me as a beach vacation kind of guy."

"And the other?"

"Mind you, I am simply speculating; however, Jada has mentioned a substantial increase in drug trafficking activity on the island. Perhaps his presence on the island has something to do with that."

"That was my thinking as well."

"Have you enlisted Jada's assistance in resolving the matter?"

"I have not."

"If you like, I could reach out to her on your behalf."

"Thank you, Mercedes. I appreciate that."

"Anything I can do for my Family, it is my privilege to perform."

"Well, if that's the case, maybe you could help me with a problem I'm having."

"As I said, anything I can do for my Family."

"How do you recruit the women to work here?"

"I recruit them in different ways and in different places." Mercedes scanned her club and pointed. "That, for example, is Adriana Carlton."

"Which one?"

"The one in the Pamella Roland floral one-shoulder gown."

"Which one?"

"The one in the black and purple dress."

"Got her."

"She used to work at the place where I used to get gas. One day, I went into the store, and she told me that she'd been admiring me and the way I dressed and the way I presented myself. When she said that she wanted to do whatever I did so she could dress and present herself the way I did, I gave her a thousand dollars."

"Hook."

"Then I took her to buy an evening gown and shoes and get her hair and makeup done. Once she was dressed appropriately, I told her to meet me here the following evening."

"Line and sinker," Carter chuckled.

"I simply introduced her to the lifestyle she wanted to live, and then I taught her how to succeed in that world."

Carter considered what Mercedes had said. "I imagine the process is the same."

"I beg your pardon?"

"I was just thinking out loud. Knuckles's wife, Kelsey, had been recruiting dancers to work their spot from my other clubs." Carter paused. "You don't recruit out of my clubs, do you?"

"No. Mainly because I'm not looking for dancers. I look for and, in turn, recruit women who walk like a lady, women who can speak clearly and carry themselves a certain way."

"I'm not sure about Fiona, but you and Fantasy were both dancers, right?"

"Jada's little clones." Mercedes giggled. "That's what Mr. Ray calls Fantasy, Fiona, and me. And no, Mr. Garrison, Fiona was not a dancer. I believe Jada met her at an album release party. Fantasy and I were indeed dancers. But Jada didn't recruit either of us, and I'm quite sure she wouldn't have. Fantasy and I were both referred to Jada by Mr. Black."

"I see. I was thinking that the solution to my Kelsey problem was for you to take over recruiting. But I see now that wouldn't work. You don't shop in the same type of store," Carter said as he saw Geno arrive at La Chat.

"I wouldn't have put it quite that way, but yes, our markets are totally different."

When Geno spotted Carter sitting at the table with Mercedes, he came to the table.

"Good evening, Mr. Crocker."

"How are you, Mercedes?"

"I'm awesome as always. Please sit," Mercedes said, signaling for one of her ladies.

"Yes, Mercedes?" Basha responded.

"Please bring Mr. Garrison and Mr. Crocker whatever they are drinking."

"Hennessy Paradis," Carter said.

"Same for me, Basha," Geno said, and she went to get their drinks.

"And now, if you'll excuse me." Mercedes stood up. "I will leave you gentlemen to your business."

"Geno!" Carter shouted like he used to when they were kids.

Geno sat down. "What's up, Carter?"

"Might be something, might be nothing."

"Okay," Geno said as Basha returned with their drinks.

"Good evening, Mr. Garrison, Mr. Crocker," Basha said, setting the drinks on the table.

Basha Marszałek was a Polish woman with fair skin, bright blue eyes, and blond hair that Mercedes recruited at an international trade convention. At the time, Basha was working as the third assistant to the Public Relations and Communications manager, which meant that her job was to get coffee and look pretty.

"Will there be anything else, gentlemen?"

"Thank you, Basha. That will be all for now," Geno said, and Basha left the table.

"Tell me, can you think of any reason other than drugs for Mitch to be in Nassau?" Carter paused. "Take your time. I'll wait."

"No. I can't think of any reason."

"Vixen said that she saw him there this weekend, and there was a shooting. She doesn't know if Mitch was involved in the shooting, but a woman was killed."

"I guess my first question would be, what was Vixen doing in Nassau?"

"She's a model, and there was a show there this weekend."

"It wouldn't have anything to do with the lovely Ms. West, would it?"

"I don't think so, but Mercedes is checking on that for me." Carter shot his drink. "What do you know about him, Geno?"

"I know Mitch pushes through a lot of merchandise, but I can't speak to whether he's dealing."

"Find out for me."

"You got it."

Chapter Seven

The following morning at ten o'clock, Carmen arrived at the studio to do the news at noon. She was so tired that she didn't go on her usual five-mile run that morning. She had spent the early part of the evening at Knuckles's spot with Victoria.

"A.k.a. Vixen," Carmen giggled.

She was surprised and relieved that nobody at Knuckles's recognized her. Carmen was able to sit at the bar and drink in peace, and she liked that because it didn't happen very often.

Who notices Carmen Taylor in a room full of naked women? Carmen thought and sat down at her desk.

Carmen hung out at Knuckles's with Vixen until after midnight. But instead of going home, she went to the mansion and hung out with Jada for a couple of hours.

"Good morning, Carmen," Stephanie Zaire said as she stuck her head in the door.

"Morning, Stephanie." Carmen waved for her to enter her office. "How was your night?"

"Good." Stephanie sat down. "I was able to reach out to Tomesia Navarro. She's the woman I told you about who says she knows the real Patsy McWalter."

"What did she say?"

"She wants to tell her story, but she won't come into the studio."

"Why not?"

"She said that the McWalters are very powerful, and they have eyes everywhere."

"That's probably true."

"And I quote: 'They know me, they don't like me, and if they found out that I was talking to the press, they would ruin my life.'"

"That's probably true too," Carmen laughed. "Her saying something that goes against the goody-two-shoes image that the family is portraying . . . No, it will not go well for her." Carmen exhaled. "So, what do we do? See if she is willing to meet you somewhere."

"I'll see what she says. Thanks, Carmen," Stephanie said, leaving Carmen's office. When she was gone, Lacara appeared in the doorway.

"Morning, Carmen."

"Hey, Lacara."

"You ready to go to work?"

"No." Carmen stood up. "But let's get to it anyway."

When Carmen returned to her office later that afternoon after doing the news, Stephanie was there waiting.

"I'm going to assume that you talked to Tomesia Navarro," Carmen said as she walked past Stephanie and went into her office. Stephanie got up and followed her in.

"Yes, I did speak to her."

Carmen sat down. "What did she say? Is she willing to meet you somewhere?"

"She is willing to meet, but she'll only talk to you."

Carmen closed her eyes and leaned back in her chair. "Why am I not surprised? Did she give you a reason why?"

"As a matter of fact, she did."

"I'm dying to hear what it is."

"She doesn't know me." Stephanie pointed at Carmen. "But she watches you every day, twice a day, so she feels like she knows you."

"You know, that kind of makes sense to me."

"It did to me too." Stephanie giggled. "And besides, she's Carmen Taylor. Who doesn't wanna meet her?"

"She said that?"

"She did."

"That's the price of fame."

"So," Stephanie paused, "what do you wanna do?"

"Arrange a meeting. Time and place, and I'll be there."

An hour later, Stephanie was back in Carmen's office. She had arranged for Carmen to meet Tomesia Navarro in Chelsea Park by the soccer field.

"How will I know her?" Carmen asked.

"She said she'll find you."

"Okay. Give me some background; who is this woman?"

"Tomesia Navarro is a 28-year-old freelance makeup artist."

"How does she know Patsy McWalter?"

"She met *Winter,* that's what she says everyone called her, at a party. I checked her social media, and there are a lot of pictures of them at different parties."

"So, she's the real thing."

"Seems like she is."

"What else you got?"

"Not much more than that."

"Okay, that will have to be enough," Carmen said and went about the rest of her day until it was time to meet Tomesia.

At two o'clock that afternoon, Carmen was sitting in the bleachers by the soccer field at Chelsea Park. She was watching the women play and had gotten so into the competition that she didn't notice when a woman sat down next to her.

"Good game?"

"Yeah, it's kind of exciting."

"I never got into soccer myself. I always thought that there was too much running around and not enough scoring."

Carmen looked at the woman and was about to ask her, *If you never got into it, why are you here watching?*

"Carmen Taylor." The woman extended her hand. "Tomesia Navarro."

Carmen smiled and shook her hand. "It's nice to meet you. Thank you for agreeing to talk to me."

"Thank you for taking me seriously."

"You're welcome. I believe that knowing the truth about her and the people she associated with would help find her killer."

"I thought the same thing."

"So, what can you tell me about Winter?"

"I guess the first thing is that she's not the innocent, good girl that her parents thought that she was." Tomesia laughed. "She had them totally fooled."

"So, you're saying that the parents believe what they're saying about their daughter," Carmen said more than asked.

"They just don't know. They never did. From the time she was in junior high."

"What happened in junior high?"

"They sent her to this really bougie private school, but there were two Black girls who went there, and that's who my girl hung out with. It was them who gave her the name 'Winter.' It was the same when she went away to college at Northwestern University. She lived off campus and hung out with the Black people, but she was smart about it. Winter would go to, you know, the events white people held, and she took pictures to post for her parents to see. She was really popular with them, so she was able to pull it off. She'd date the occasional white boy, but that was just to keep up appearances." She chuckled. "But Winter had a thing for bad boys."

Carmen chuckled. "Why am I not surprised?"

"The worse a man was for her, the more she'd love them."

"Any of them violent that you know of?"

"There was one. His name was Anton Moore."

"What can you tell me about him?"

"That he was an asshole." She laughed. "And he sold drugs. Opioids mostly, but he dabbled in cocaine sometimes."

"You know where I can find him?"

"I've probably got his number somewhere. I'll look for it."

"So, Winter did drugs."

"Yes, she most certainly did. And she liked to party," Tomesia paused. "You should come to a party with me."

"I don't think that's a good idea," Carmen said, and then she thought about it. "But then again, I could wear a disguise, like a wig."

"Winter liked wigs too."

"And not ask a lot of questions." Carmen nodded. "That might work."

"Great." Tomesia smiled. "If you have time, I can show you the duality that was Winter."

"How so?"

"Her condo isn't far from here."

Carmen glanced at her watch. "I've got time." She stood up. "Let's go."

It didn't take long for them to get to Winter's condo. Her family owned the West Nineteenth Street property, and, in their mourning, they hadn't been there since her murder. Therefore, the unit was precisely as Winter left it.

"This might sound like a stupid question, but I'm gonna go with it anyway," Carmen began as they got off the elevator and walked down the hall. "How are we going to get in?" she asked, but Carmen was fully prepared to pick the lock if necessary. It was a skill that she learned and mastered when she was dating Mike Black.

"I have a key," Tomesia said as they arrived at the door.

She unlocked the door, turned off the alarm, and they went into the fabulously decorated space. She led Carmen to Winter's bedroom.

"There are two closets." She pointed to the door on the left. "That's Patsy's closet. Go ahead," she encouraged. "Take a look."

Carmen opened the door to the walk-in closet and stepped inside. The closet was filled with designer clothes. Dresses, pantsuits, shoes, and all of the outfits were very conservative; some might say that they were on the prudish side. Tomesia stepped into the closet.

"She did love shoes," she giggled. "Come on."

Carmen followed Tomesia out of the Patsy closet and watched as she opened the other closet door with a flourish. She and Carmen stepped inside, and the difference was stark.

"This is Winter's closet."

"Wow."

Once again, the closet was filled to the point of overflowing with outfits from the world's finest designers. However, where the Patsy closet contained a collection of very conservative, borderline prudish outfits, the dresses, suits, and shoes in the Winter closet were more flamboyant and provocative. There was an entire section dedicated to jeans. There was an elaborate collection of wigs and a cosmetics area.

"I see what you mean," Carmen said and followed Tomesia out of the closet.

"I know you have to go, but let me show you two more things," she said, taking out her phone. She went on Instagram. "This is Patsy's page."

She handed the phone to Carmen, and she scrolled through the images. All of the photos were of her dressed in those conservative outfits in different places with different people. There were many images of her with her parents.

"Where were these taken?"

"At Mommy and Daddy's golf club." Carmen handed her back the phone. "Now, check out Winter's page."

Carmen scrolled through the images, and the difference, once again, was stark.

"See what I mean?"

"Yes. Mommy and Daddy had no idea who their daughter really was."

"That's why the police have no leads or even a suspect. They aren't talking to the people who actually *knew* her."

Chapter Eight

Eugene Crooker considered himself to be a fortunate man, and he believed that it was because Carter Garrison was his best friend. He was lucky to be standing in the back of the line in front of Carter when they were in kindergarten. He felt lucky that they grew up best friends. It was Carter who tagged him with the name "Geno" when they were in the third grade. Geno and Carter did just about everything together. So, when Carter bagged up an ounce of weed to sell, Geno said, "I'm all in."

And Geno was in a few years later when Carter suggested that they step up to cocaine.

One night, that luck ran out for Carter when the police came for them. They ran and thought that they had gotten away.

"Stop, police!"

With the police in pursuit, they ran until they reached a fence. Geno hit the fence first and made it over, but not Carter. Just as he reached the top, the police grabbed him. Geno stopped and looked back at Carter.

"Go!" Carter yelled as the police pulled him down.

Carter was arrested and charged with possession with intent to distribute. When the cops tried to get him to identify who was with him, Carter kept his mouth shut. He pleaded guilty to simple possession and was sentenced to two years.

Geno had everything set up and ready for Carter to walk into when he got out, but he wasn't interested.

While he was in jail, Carter got in with some people who had a job waiting for him working for Mike Black, and suggested that Geno get in with him. But Geno was making money and saw no reason to give it up.

When the game dried up, Geno found a new hustle. He knew people who wanted something that they were willing to pay for, and Carter knew plenty of people who had goods and services to sell. It was just a matter of putting the two together. From there, Geno built a reputation for being the guy who could get you whatever your heart desired if you were willing to pay for it. After several sharp turns, uphills, closed doors, and setbacks over the years, Geno had a successful fencing business, and he was Carter's top lieutenant.

What Geno was not lucky at was love. However, tales of Sabrina McMillan and Valencia DeVerão were in the past, and that is where Geno preferred to keep them.

That morning, Geno was at the offices of Invulnerable Security. It was one of The Family's legitimate businesses that was engaged in providing guard and patrol services, bodyguards, and private investigators.

Carter had tasked him with finding Mitch and what he was into. When you needed somebody found, the people you called were Angel and Bowie. But Geno knew that although Angel and Bowie would provide him with the information he needed, they were killers, and for the time being, he needed Mitch alive. Therefore, he was at Invulnerable to hire an investigator to follow Mitch.

His name was Albert Nitty, and he was the best investigator in the company. What made Nitty so good at his job was his ability to blend in. Since Geno couldn't tell Nitty where to find Mitch, he planned to stake out his apartment and wait for him to show up.

"I'll pick him up there," Nitty promised. "I'll call you and let you know when I get him."

"Sounds good."

Now that Geno had Nitty on task, he turned his attention to finding out what Mitch was into. He knew that Mitch ran a robbing crew with a guy named Welch. Mitch had brought him along one night when he had something to sell. He also knew that Welch hung out at a billiard hall called Balls and Sticks.

Geno walked into the billiard hall and looked around for Welch, thinking it would be nice if Mitch were there. That way, he could call Nitty and have him pick up surveillance of Mitch from there. He didn't see Mitch anywhere, but Welch was there shooting pool. Geno approached the table.

"Your name is Welch, right?"

"Yeah, who's asking?" Welch turned and looked at Geno. He recognized him as Mitch's fence.

"I am."

"You're Geno, right?"

"Right."

"We met one night with Mitch."

Geno looked closely at Welch and nodded. "That's right. He around? I need to talk to him about a job."

Welch chuckled. "Knowing how Mitch likes to brag, I'm not surprised you think that he runs the crew."

Geno chuckled. "He's not?"

"Hell no. This is *my* crew."

"Then you're the man I need to be talking to."

"Yeah, I'm thinking that you do. What's up?"

"I got a job that needs to get done tomorrow."

"That's short notice."

Geno chuckled. "Mitch led me to believe that short notice was no problem."

"It's not, but tomorrow doesn't leave a lot of time for planning, and that's how niggas get themselves locked up."

Welch looked around.

"Dana!" he shouted, and a woman who was shooting pool looked up. He waved her over. She held up one finger and finished her shot.

"Eight ball, side pocket."

When the eight ball went into the side pocket, Dana put down her stick and held out her hand.

"Pay me."

Once she had her money, she joined them at the table. Dana English stood five feet six inches, with deep chocolate skin and long skinny braids that hung down her back. Geno watched her as she walked toward them and liked what he saw.

"What's up?" she asked when she got to the table.

"Dana, this is Geno." He pointed, and Dana's eyes opened wide. "Yeah, the Geno," Welch said, and Dana got excited.

"Nice to meet you, Geno. We've been wanting to meet you for a long time," she said, looking over Geno from head to toe.

She liked what she saw.

Geno stepped closer to Dana. "And why is that?" he asked.

"Shit," Welch began, "you're the only reason we fucked with Mitch."

"Because he had access to you," Dana added, taking a step closer to Geno. She looked up into his eyes.

"Wait a minute." Geno could feel the heat emanating from Dana's body. "He wasn't even part of your crew, was he?"

"Nope." Dana paused. "I mean, we might use him if we were a man short, but no. Mitch had other shit going."

"Like what?"

"Like everybody and his pops, your boy's trying to step up and make some moves in the dope game," Dana said, and Geno nodded.

"Geno said he's got a job for us, but it's gotta go down tomorrow."

"Short window," Dana commented.

"Mitch told him that wouldn't be a problem."

"Bastard." Dana shook her head in disgust. She neither liked nor had any respect for Mitch. He was simply a means to an end. "What's the job?"

"Warehouse in Red Hook."

"What's the product?" she asked.

"Flat screens fresh off the boat from China. They'll be stored in that warehouse and distributed the day after."

"Can we see the warehouse?"

"You in or not?"

"Oh, we're most definitely in," Welch said, and Dana gave him the side eye. She didn't want to commit to doing the job sight unseen, but she went along with her partner anyway.

"Good. Let's go see the warehouse," Geno said, and Welch and Dana followed him out of Balls and Sticks.

Even though Dana had told him that Mitch was involved in the drug game, as everybody suspected, the job was real. He got the tip the night before and was going to put a crew together to take the warehouse, but this was even better. If Dana, Welch, and their crew were any good, and he assumed from his experience with Mitch that they were, he would have work for them. Geno ran across jobs all the time. Having a crew on standby to do the jobs that he ran across would be excellent.

When they arrived in Red Hook, Dana checked out the property from the roof of the building across the street. She took out some binoculars and surveyed the property.

"I'm guessing they got security out the wazoo," she commented.

"They do."

"Can you offer any insight into what level of security they have?"

"Three armed guards. One at the gate," Geno said, and Dana spotted him with binoculars. "One at the loading dock and the other floats. He checks in with either the gate or the loading dock every twenty minutes. Is that gonna be a problem?"

"No. No problem," Dana said confidently.

Welch chuckled and pointed at Dana. "My girl here is the best hacker in the business."

"I know a couple of people who would give her some stiff competition for that title."

"Maybe," Dana said, stepping closer to Geno and looking up into his eyes. "But I guarantee you that I'll have the system down pat by the time we're ready to go to work."

Geno took a step closer to Dana and looked down into her eyes.

"I like a woman with confidence," he said as his phone vibrated with a text message. He took out the phone and glanced at the display. It was from Nitty.

I got him.

Dana looked at Welch. "I think we need another man for this."

"I agree," Welch said.

"You gonna call Mitch?" Geno asked, and they both looked at him. It was as if Mitch wouldn't have been their first choice.

"We could," Welch said. Dana took out her phone and made the call.

"Hello," Mitch answered.

"We got a job to do tomorrow. You interested?"

"Yeah, yeah, count me in."

"Meet us at the pool hall around ten, and we'll go from there."

"Cool. See you tomorrow." Mitch ended the call and got his gun.

He had only just recently returned from The Bahamas, which turned out to be a total waste of time, and it almost got him killed. He knew that it wouldn't take long for them to send people after him. What he wasn't expecting was for them to see him in The Bahamas.

But he should have.

Mitch was glad to hear from Dana about a job. He knew it wasn't gonna be enough to cover his debt, but it would bring him a step closer to having it. Mitch looked out the window before he left the apartment.

Nitty was parked down the street from Mitch's apartment, and he saw him when he exited the building. He took a few pictures of him walking to and getting in his car. He started it up, and when Mitch drove off, he followed.

Mitch went to a meeting with two men at The System, and Nitty got pictures of him going inside. He waited for a minute before he entered the building. Nitty looked around the crowded club and spotted Mitch at the bar. He was involved in a heated discussion with a woman. Nitty took a picture of the two as they got in each other's faces. Nitty got a great picture when the woman slapped the shit out of Mitch, spit in his face, and walked away. He was about to go after her when two men came up behind Mitch and grabbed his arms.

Nitty got some great shots of the two men escorting Mitch out of The System. He hurried to keep up as they hustled him to their car. When they reached the vehicle, one man looked around before he opened the trunk and tossed Mitch in. Once they closed the trunk and got in, Nitty had to run to his car so he could follow them.

When he made it to his vehicle, Nitty followed them to a place called The Hole in the Wall. He watched and captured images of the men taking Mitch out of the trunk and walking him through the back door. Then Nitty took out his phone and made a call.

"This is Carla."

"Good evening, Carla. My name is Albert Nitty. I'm an investigator with Invulnerable Security doing an assignment for Geno Crocker."

"Yes, Mr. Nitty, what can I do for you?"

"I've got some images that I'd like you to run facial recognition on."

"No problem, Mr. Nitty. Send them over."

"Thank you, Carla."

"When I get a match, would you like me to send the information to Geno as well?"

"I would greatly appreciate it," Nitty answered.

"Consider it done. I will be expecting those images."

"You should have them shortly. Thanks again, Carla."

"No worries."

Carla ended the call, and when she received the images, she called Geno. He was still with Dana when she called. Geno glanced at the display and saw it was Carla calling.

"Would you excuse me a moment? I need to take this call."

"Sure."

Geno got up and stepped away from the table. "What's up, Carla?"

"Hey, Geno. I just wanted to let you know that I got the images from Nitty, and I'm running facial recognition on them."

"Thanks, Carla."

"It's going to take awhile."

"Call me when you get something." Geno thought for a moment. "Hey, Carla. Send me those images, will you?"

"Will do," she replied and forwarded them from Nitty to Geno. When Geno got them, he looked at them before sending them to Carter, and then he called him.

"Geno, what's up?"

"I just sent you some pictures."

"I just got them. Hold on." Carter looked at the images of the two men putting Mitch in the trunk.

"I was thinking that those might be the guys from Nassau."

"I was thinking the same thing," Carter said. "I'll roll by Club Envy and show these to Vixen. Where are you?"

"I'm at Balls and Sticks."

"What are you doing there?"

Geno looked at Dana. She smiled and waved, and he waved back. "I'll tell you when I see you," he said, still looking at her.

"Cool."

Geno ended the call and went back to talking to Dana while Carter headed for Club Envy. After stopping in the office and speaking with Vanessa, Carter went out on the floor to look for Vixen. When he saw her, she was on her way to dance on the main stage. Carter took a seat and watched her as Vixen went to work.

She is pretty, he thought and agreed with Carmen that Victoria Howard, a.k.a. Vixen, was meant for bigger things than stripping in a room full of men and shaking her ass for their entertainment. When her third song, a slow, sensual track, began, Carter stood up and took a twenty-dollar bill from his pocket. He approached the stage and waited with the other men.

He handed her the bill. "We need to talk when you get finished up here."

Vixen took the bill and put it in her garter. "Okay," she said and danced away from him.

Once she finished her set, Vixen returned to the dressing room to change. When she came back out on the floor, she walked around and thanked the men who tipped her on stage. Then she looked around for Carter. She spotted him at a table in the back of Club Envy.

"Hey, Carter." She sat down at the table with him. "You wanted to see me?"

"Yeah." Carter took out his phone. "I wanted you to look at some images."

"Okay."

He handed her the phone, and she looked at the photos.

"You recognize them?"

"Yes." She looked again closely. "Those are the two guys I saw Mitch with at the bar in Nassau."

Chapter Nine

It was getting late in the afternoon when Geno got a call from Carla. She asked if he could come to the office because she had some important information to share with him. Geno promised to be there within the hour. When he arrived in the lobby, Carla met him and escorted Geno to her office.

"What you got for me, Carla?"

"Their names are Telvin Henderson and James Bellamy. They're muscle for a drug dealer named Winston Townson. He works for Modesto Colbert."

It was a few hours later when Winston Townson opened the door to the storage room at The Hole in the Wall and walked in. Bellamy and Henderson had Mitch gagged and tied to a chair. They had been there waiting for Townson to arrive since the night before.

"Sorry it took me so long to get here. I had important shit to take care of." He walked up to Mitch in the chair. "Why you two got my man Mitch tied up like that?" He took the gag out of his mouth and looked at Henderson and Bellamy. "Untie him."

While they untied Mitch, Townson walked out of the storage room and went out to the bar. He ordered a drink for himself. When Mitch came out of the storage room, he was rubbing his wrists and was happy to be still alive. He sat down at the bar next to Townson.

"You all right, buddy?"

Mitch glanced at Henderson and Bellamy. "I'm okay."

"Good. Good. You wanna drink?"

"Whiskey."

Instead of having the bartender fix the drink, Townson stood up and went behind the bar.

"What kind of whiskey are you drinking, brother?"

"Doesn't matter. Bar brand is fine."

"Fuck no." Townson grabbed a bottle of Glenfiddich Single Malt 23-Year-Old Grand Cru. He held up the bottle for all to see. "Nothing but top shelf for my man here."

Townson poured the liquor into two glasses and slipped a pill laced with cyanide into Mitch's drink and handed it to him. Mitch drank it down quickly, and Townson poured him another.

"You good?" Townson asked.

Once again, Mitch looked at Henderson and Bellamy. "Yeah, man, I'm okay."

"Good. Good. Now, tell me, what's happening with my money?"

"I just got back from Nassau. I was down there trying to find out what happened."

"And?"

"Somebody fucked up."

Townson nodded. "You damn right somebody fucked up."

"I just need another week to come up with the money. I got something going down tomorrow."

"That's all fine and dandy, Mitch, it really is, but you ain't gonna make it," Townson said, and he started laughing when Mitch began sweating.

Mitch looked confused. "Why not?"

"Because you're going to be dead soon," he said as Mitch grabbed his chest.

Mitch quickly stood up. "I don't feel so good," he said, becoming dizzy.

Suddenly, his heart rate increased, and Mitch began having difficulty breathing. He grabbed his chest and fell to the floor.

Townson stood over him. "What's wrong, buddy?"

As nearby customers looked on in horror, Mitch started to convulse as if he were having a seizure.

"You all right, Mitch?" Townson asked, laughing.

He vomited, his breath got short, and soon after, Mitch stopped breathing.

"Get rid of the body and clean that nasty shit up," Townson told Bellamy and Henderson, and he left The Hole in the Wall to the sound of Mitch's cell phone ringing.

"He's not answering," Dana said and put her phone away.

She was at Balls and Sticks with Geno, Welch, and another man she had brought in for the job. He was dressed in a security guard's uniform.

"We need another man," Welch said.

"No," Dana said emphatically. "We can handle it."

"It's a four-man job," Welch replied.

"I *said* we can handle it," Dana said emphatically.

Welch held up his hand in surrender. "Okay," he reluctantly agreed.

Dana stood up. "Let's go," she said and led her crew out of Balls and Sticks.

Welch got into the truck he had stolen with Geno. Dana and the other man got in her car, and they headed for the warehouse. When they arrived, she parked, and as the man hung back, she approached the gate.

"Can I help you?" the guard said.

"No. But he has something for you," Dana said as the other man came up behind the guard and hit him with a stun gun.

The man dragged the guard behind the security shack, put plastic cuffs on his wrists and ankles, and gagged him. Dana went into the security shack and opened the gate. Welch drove through the gate, and Geno got out to wait for the floating security guard. Dana got into the truck and went around to the dock with Welch. When the guard saw the vehicle coming, he checked his clipboard for late-night deliveries or pickups.

There were none scheduled.

He got up and walked to the truck. He watched as Welch got out of the vehicle and came up on the dock.

"How's it going?" Welch asked.

"What are you doing here? You're not on the schedule," the guard said as Dana came up behind him and stuck a gun in his back.

"I don't wanna kill you, and you don't wanna be dead. Now, I'm gonna take your gun, and then you're gonna lie down on the ground with your fingers interlaced behind your head. Nod if you understand."

When the guard nodded, Dana took his gun, and he lay down on the ground as instructed.

"Good man."

While Welch cuffed and gagged the guard, Dana noticed that there was another truck at the dock. Geno had taken care of the floating guard and had just arrived at the pier when Dana opened the truck.

"Hey, Geno, come here."

Geno walked over to her. "What's up?"

Dana pointed. "This one is already loaded. I say we take it and get outta here. What do you think?"

"Where are the keys?"

Dana took out her gun and approached the guard. She put the gun to his head.

"Where are the keys?" Dana asked, and he tried to answer through the gag. "Take the gag out of his mouth."

Welch removed the gag. "They're in the shack on the board."

"Thank you." Dana got the keys and tossed them to Welch. "Let's get outta here."

"What about the truck?" Welch asked, pointing to the truck they came in.

"Wipe it down and leave it," she ordered. "It's stolen anyway."

Once Welch wiped down the truck for fingerprints, they got in the other vehicle, picked up their man at the gate, and drove away.

It was after five in the morning, and Nitty was still parked outside of The Hole in the Wall. He had been there since Henderson and Bellamy dragged Mitch inside. Townson had left hours ago. He could see the front and back doors from where he was parked, so he knew they hadn't come out.

At five thirty, the back door opened, and Bellamy came out. He walked to his car and backed as close to the door as he could. Then he went back inside. A few minutes later, the door opened again, and Nitty watched Bellamy and Henderson carry out something big and put it in the trunk of Bellamy's car. Then they got in the vehicle and drove away, with Nitty following at a safe distance. They went to the Hudson River, removed what they had from the trunk, and tossed it in the river.

At precisely nine o'clock the following morning, Geno's phone began ringing. "Hello."

"It's Nitty. Can we meet somewhere?"

"Yeah. Meet me at George's Diner on Westchester in twenty minutes."

"See you there."

When Geno arrived at the diner, Nitty was eating pancakes with bacon and sipping coffee. Geno sat down at the table.

"What's up with Mitch?"

"I can't be sure, but I think Mitch is sleeping with the fish."

Chapter Ten

Carter was asleep when his phone started ringing that morning. His eyes sprang open, and he reached for the phone.

"Hello."

"It's Geno. Sorry to bother you, but we need to talk."

"Where are you?"

"George's Diner on Westchester."

"Okay. I'll be there in twenty minutes."

Carter ended the call and dragged himself out of bed.

"You gotta go?" his female companion for the night asked.

"Yeah."

Carter kissed her on the cheek, and then he quickly showered, dressed, left the hotel, and was on his way. When he arrived at the diner, Geno was eating a Belgian waffle and sausage.

"When you invite somebody to breakfast," Carter sat down, "it's customary to wait until they arrive to start eating."

"You're right. When I got here, Nitty was gobbling up some pancakes, and I got hungry, so I ordered some waffles."

"No worries. What's up?" Carter asked as the server approached.

"Good morning, sir." She handed Carter a menu. "What can I start you with?" she asked, refilling Geno's coffee.

"I'll have the steak and eggs. Well done, with cheddar and Swiss cheese," he said, handing her the menu.

"Coffee?"

"Please."

She turned over his cup and poured Carter some coffee. "I'll have that out for you soon," she promised before she left the table.

"So, what's up with Mitch?"

"Nitty says he can't be sure, but he thinks Mitch is 'sleeping with the fish.'"

Carter laughed at the reference to *The Godfather, part one*. "He actually said that?"

"He did," Geno said and relayed the information he got from Nitty. "He said that they took what he said looked like a body out of the trunk and tossed it into the river."

"I'm betting that was Mitch," Carter said as his food arrived.

"What you gonna do?"

"Right now, I'm gonna eat," he said and dug into the steak.

Geno ate his waffle and sipped coffee, while Carter ate his. When he finished, he paid the check, and they left the diner together.

"So, what you gonna do?" Geno asked as they walked to their cars.

"I'll let you know," Carter said and got into his car.

As he drove away from George's Diner, Carter was torn about what to do next.

Now that he knew that Mitch was involved with Winston Townson in the drug business, he would have killed him for what he was doing because it went against Mike Black's rule.

No drugs.

End of story.

However, Mitch was still a member of The Family. Winston Townson had a member of The Family killed, and protocol demanded that Carter do something about it. He knew the thing to do was to call Rain, but he didn't feel like being bothered with her one or two-word answers. He needed advice, so he took out his phone and made a call.

Mike Black had just gotten out of the pool when his phone began ringing. The Blacks had a fifty-meter pool, and Black liked to swim laps when the weather permitted.

"Good morning, Mr. Garrison."

"Morning, Mike. Sorry to bother you so early, but I need to talk to you."

"I'm at the house. Come on out."

"I'm on my way."

Black ended the call and put down the phone. He opened a bottle of water and took a drink. As he was putting down the bottle, Michelle was coming out of the house wearing a Dolce & Gabbana one-piece halter swimsuit. He shook his head at the sight of his baby girl.

"Morning, Daddy."

"Morning. You getting in?"

"Yup," Michelle said, and she dove in.

Michelle was practically raised on the beach in The Bahamas, so, like her father, she loved the water. Black watched her as she swam a few laps. She had good form. When she finished with her laps, she got out and dried herself.

"Carter Garrison is on his way out here to talk," Black told his daughter when she sat down beside him.

"Can I stay?"

"Yes. But keep your mouth shut. If you have any questions, comments, opinions, or suggestions about what he says, we'll talk about it later."

"I'm good with that."

"Cool."

"And I won't tell Mommy."

"You can tell her if you want to. She's coming to grips with the fact that her baby isn't a baby anymore, and she is becoming more accepting of your position and your future in this Family."

"Thank you, Daddy."

"For what?"

"For everything, but specifically for talking to Mommy."

"I don't know if you've met your mother, but she's hard to avoid."

"Tell me about it," Michelle said, thinking that Shy may be coming to grips with it, but she still treated her like a little girl at times.

Michelle stood up.

"Where are you going?"

"To put on a coverall." Michelle struck a pose. "All this ain't for everybody to see," she said and went toward the house.

"Thank God," Black said, shaking his head as she walked away.

When Carter arrived at Black's house, he stopped at the gate. Roland stepped out of the guard shack and held up his hand.

"State your business."

"Carter Garrison to see Mike Black. He's expecting me."

Roland nodded his head, and the gate opened. "Have a good day, Mr. Garrison," he said, and Carter drove through the gate. When he got to the house, William came outside and met him at the car, opening the door.

"Morning, Mr. Garrison."

"Morning, William."

"The boss is waiting for you at the pool," William said, and he led Carter into the house and escorted him to the pool.

When Carter came out onto the pool deck, Black and Michelle stood up. She was wearing a ViX by Paula Hermanny Perola short cover-up robe over her swimsuit.

Carter was surprised when he saw Michelle standing in what she considered her rightful place at her father's side. He had heard that one day, they would all be working for Michelle. But he merely took it as mere speculation.

"What up, Carter?" Black shook hands with him.

"How are you, Mike?"

"I'm good."

"How are you doing, Michelle?"

"I'm doing fine, Mr. Garrison."

"Have a seat," Black said.

"Thanks." Carter sat.

When Michelle sat down next to Black, Carter looked at her.

I guess it's more than just talk.

"What's going on?" Black asked.

"One of our dancers said that she saw Mitch in Nassau."

"What was he doing there?" Black asked.

"Yet to be determined. But I have Carmen Taylor and Mercedes checking to see if Jada knows anything about it."

"What does Carmen have to do with this?" Black asked because he was extremely protective of her.

"The dancer, Vixen. Carmen is trying to get her into modeling. That's what she was doing there. There was a fashion show in Nassau, and a shooting took place at the show."

Michelle looked at Black. She wanted to say something so badly, but she had given her word that she would keep her mouth shut.

"Was Mitch involved in the shooting?"

"I don't know. But I had Geno look into Mitch. He had an Invulnerable investigator follow Mitch. He was picked up and tossed into the trunk of a car by two men. Their names are Telvin Henderson and James Bellamy. They're muscle for a drug dealer named Winston Townson; he works for Modesto Colbert."

"I've heard the names. Go on."

"The investigator, Nitty, saw them put what looked like a body in the trunk, and then he followed them to the Hudson River, where they took what they had out of the trunk and tossed it into the river." Carter chuckled. "Nitty said he thinks Mitch 'sleeps with the fish.'"

Michelle smiled, and Black chuckled. "Pretty safe bet."

"I was gonna kill Mitch for being involved in the drug business, but they beat me to it. But Mitch was a member of this Family, so I need to do something about it."

"Rid the world of one more drug dealer." Black laughed. "But you're right. Mitch was a Family member. Wouldn't look good if we did nothing."

"I'll get it done. But I'm not interested in starting a war over somebody I was gonna kill anyway. I was thinking Monika would be a good choice."

"I agree. But Monika is out of the country. I have no idea where in the world she is. She just told me she was gone and would call me when she got back. But you're right; having a snipper handle this from a distance would be better than sending men after him."

"And Fantasy is in Nassau."

"Talk to Jackie."

"Jackie?"

"Yeah. Jackie used to be a part of Colonel Mathis's little band of assassins. She's good with a long gun. She's not as good as Monika, but she can line up and hit a shot from a distance."

"A woman of many talents," Carter said, nodding his head. "I'll reach out to her tonight."

Michelle stood up. “If you gentlemen would excuse me, I have to get ready for a meeting. It was good to see you, Mr. Garrison.”

“Nice to see you too. I hear you and Barbara are doing big things.”

“We’re trying to do a little something.” She glanced at her father. “Do you have any plans for later, Daddy?”

“I’m not going anywhere.”

“Then you’ll be here when I get back?”

“I should.”

“Good. We’ll talk then,” Michelle said and walked toward the house.

Carter shook his head. “They grow up so fast. I still remember her screaming her head off at Shy’s funeral.”

“So do I.” Black watched Michelle go into the house. “What’s going on with you and Rain?”

“She’s speaking to me. And she’s used me a couple of times when she needed muscle.”

“That’s a start. It was starting to affect our business.”

“I know.”

“You all right?”

“I am now. But I’ll be honest with you, that baby shit had me fucked up for more than a minute.” Carter chuckled. “That and the way she cut me off.”

“I heard Rain slinging some powerful shit.”

Carter shook his head. “She is,” he said, thinking about how insane the pussy was and how much he missed going up in Rain.

“Well, you know what they say?”

“What’s that?”

“The only way to get over a woman is to replace her with new pussy.”

“Trust me, Mike. I’ve been fucking everything with a pulse.” Carter shook his head. “All it does after a while is pass the time.” He stood up.

"Maybe what you need is something more than just some new pussy." Black stood up. "Find one who holds your attention." He walked Carter into the house. "And she isn't a murderer," he chuckled.

"Right. Where is she?"

"She's around here somewhere, just waiting for you to take her," Black said, and he showed him to the door.

"One more thing I wanna talk to you about."

"What's that?"

"I told you that I ran into Carmen Taylor at Knuckle's spot."

"Yeah. What was she doing there?"

"She was there to see one of the dancers. Her name is Victoria Howard, but she dances under the name Vixen."

"She's the one who saw Mitch in Nassau, right?"

"Correct."

"There was a time when I knew every dancer who worked for me." Black chuckled. "Fucked most of them. But now . . ." He shook his head. "Now, I couldn't tell you any of their names, much less fucking a bunch of them."

"A fact that I'm sure Shy appreciates."

"She does."

"Anyway, Vixen is model-quality beautiful, and Carmen would like to sponsor her so she could pursue modeling full time."

"Carmen has helped a bunch of women get started in modeling over the years. What's the problem?"

"Vixen says it's a handout, and she turned Carmen down."

"It's not a handout, it's help."

"I figured what she needs is a real job."

Black nodded. "I'll call Erykah in the morning and tell her to find her something at Prestige."

"And it needs to pay her enough money for her to give up dancing."

"I get it, Carter. But I'm curious."

"In?"

"What's your interest here?"

"None. Just trying to help make a dream come true."

"I hear you. What's the point of having power and influence if you don't wield it wisely? I'll take care of it."

"Thanks, Mike."

Chapter Eleven

After Carter left the house, Black swam a couple more laps before he went inside. Michelle was just about to leave when he came in.

"Have a good day."

"I will. And you are gonna be home when I get back, right?"

"Unless something happens, I plan to be here. And I'll text you if I leave."

Michelle kissed her father on the cheek. "Thank you, Daddy," she said and left the house.

Black went upstairs to his room and showered. He had just gotten dressed when Shy burst into the room, mumbling.

"Hello."

"Michael, you startled me."

"Sorry. I didn't mean to. But I am surprised to see you. I thought you had meetings all day."

"I did. But after that first meeting, I told Elisa to reschedule this afternoon's meeting, and here I am."

Black took Shy in his arms. "I'm guessing this morning's meeting was why you came in here, mumbling."

"Yes. Some people just have a talent for getting on my last nerve. And Emmanuele Santoro is one of those people."

Shy and Pooja had spent days preparing for that morning's meeting with Santoro. He was a shoe manufacturer looking for a new US distributor. They had worked meticulously on a pricing strategy and provided complete and accurate quotations. Therefore, Shy and Pooja knew that the implementation of various tariffs on imported goods had raised the average price of imported goods significantly. However, they had also determined the export landed costs, along with all the tariffs and taxes. They worked meticulously on a pricing strategy and provided complete and accurate quotations. The two women understood what they wanted to achieve and had taken steps to make sure both parties' interests were met.

Pooja had looked into market conditions, trends, and opportunities and researched average prices and quality standards. Her research included a consideration of cultural differences, taking into account regional and country differences, as well as communication issues like language, gestures, and facial expressions.

They were ready to close the deal.

"The meeting started at nine, and it should have taken no more than an hour or so. But no. *Three* hours. *Three* hours, Michael. Mr. Emmanuele Santoro asked a nitpicky question after a nitpicky question." Shy shook her head and imitated Santoro's annoying voice. *"I'm sorry, Mrs. Black. I'm not sure I understand that point, Mrs. Black. Could you go over that again, Mrs. Black?"*

"Michael, I got so tired of him saying, 'Could you go over it again?' I was ready to get my Beretta and put two in his head."

"Easy, Gangster," Black said, laughing.

"I need a vacation."

"You just came back from vacation, remember?"

"Yes, Michael, I remember that we just came back from vacation. But that was a family vacation. One where we spent the majority of our time with Michelle."

"True. She was our third wheel the entire time we were there."

"Right. I need a just-you-and-me vacation. No kids, no Golden Girls, just us."

"You serious?"

"Yes, Michael, I am deadly serious. It doesn't have to be long. Three or four days, maybe."

"You have anywhere in mind that you wanna go?"

"No, not really. Someplace warm."

"Islands?"

"That's fine. As long as it's just us, I don't care where we go."

Black thought for a second or two. "Let me ask you a question."

"Shoot," Shy said and began coming out of the lapel jacket that she had selected specially for that occasion. Then she kicked off her patent leather pumps.

"Did you wanna go somewhere that you could do some sightseeing and shop?"

"Sightseeing is your thing, and regardless of popular opinion, I do *not* need to shop."

"Great. Then I know just the place."

"Tell me more," she said.

She sat down on the bed and settled into Black's strong and loving arms. Shy always felt safe, protected, and comforted in those arms.

"It's a beachfront property."

"I like it already."

"It's got a private pool with semiprivate beach access, private chef, and maid service."

"I like that even better. Where is this place?"

"Our house in Freeport."

"*Really,* Michael?"

"Really, Cassandra. Think about it. No kids, no Golden Girls, no Family business, just us. Our own pool, and you know that beach is *not* crowded with tourists."

"You know I hate that."

"I know you do. We bring in Chef to cook for us. So, what do you say?"

"It sounds good, but you know as well as I do that as soon as you show your face on that island, Napoleon will have 300 things that he just *has* to show you."

"We won't let anybody know we're on the island."

"How are you gonna do that? As soon as the jet touches down, somebody at the airport will call Napoleon. I've seen it happen too many times *not* to know that's what's gonna happen."

"You let me worry about that, Mrs. Black. I'll make all the arrangements. All you gotta do is say yes."

"Yes."

"Great."

"Now, just that quickly, I'm excited about this. Just the two of us. Alone." She kissed him. "You might be in trouble, Mr. Black."

"Why is that?"

"Because I have a lot of pent-up energy and anxiety that I need to release."

"And now, just that quickly, *I'm* excited about this."

Chapter Twelve

"Thanks for joining Action News *at noon. We'll have much more news for you today at five.* The View *is up next. But keep it here for updates on the hour. I'm Carmen Taylor. And I'll see you around the city."*

"And we're out. Good job, Carmen. Great show, everybody," Lacara said.

"Thank you, Lacara."

It had been a couple of days since Carmen had spoken to Tomesia Navarro about Patsy McWalter. And in that time, she'd had an opportunity to talk with some of the people she told her about. They all painted "Winter," as she was called, in the same manner: a party girl who liked to get high and had terrible taste in men.

That afternoon, Carmen was meeting Tomesia Navarro and three other women at a nearby restaurant called Fondue. In this dining experience, the food is prepared according to your tastes with artisan cheese blends, lobster, and steak. When she arrived at the restaurant that served heated pots of cheese, chocolate, or broth for dipping, Tomesia and the other ladies were already there, waiting. They rose to their feet when they saw Carmen coming toward the table.

"Hey, Carmen," Tomesia said, and she hugged her.

"Hey," Carmen said and sat down.

"Carmen Taylor, this is Rosaland Brooks, Dominica Parker, and Bailey Griffen."

"Thank you, ladies, for agreeing to speak with me."

"Thank you, Ms. Taylor, for caring enough to wanna talk to us," Dominica said.

"Finding out the truth is never a problem, and it's Carmen." She helped herself to the Bourbon Bacon Cheddar broth for dipping. "So, what can you tell me about Winter?" Carmen asked.

"Winter was cool people," Bailey began. "She always had a smile on her face."

"I don't think I've ever seen her mad," Tomesia added.

"I have, more than once," Bailey laughed. "But even then, she didn't stay mad for very long, and she'd do everything she could to have peace of mind."

"And she'd do anything for you," Rosaland said.

"She sure would," Bailey concurred.

"I remember this one time I was short on my rent," Rosaland shared. "And I needed $1,200 to cover it. Winter wrote me a check for $2,500."

"She did me the same way," Dominica said. "And don't even think about trying to pay her back."

"I tried to pay her back once," Tomesia said, shaking her head. "And she wouldn't take it. So, you know, slick ass me, I put the money where I knew she'd find it, and I left." She giggled. "The next day, she took the money I left for her, and she got me a gift that cost what I left for her."

"That's just the way she was," Dominica said.

"Can any of you think of anybody who might have a reason to want her dead?" Carmen asked.

"No. Like I said, Winter was cool people," Dominica stated.

"I can't think of anybody who would want to kill her," Bailey said.

"Have any of you spoken to the police?" Carmen asked.

"I did," Tomesia said. "But they told me I had nothing to add, and I didn't. I couldn't tell them who killed her, so they thanked me for my time and hustled me outta there."

"What about men?" Carmen asked.

"Winter had the worst taste in men," Dominica said, and the other women agreed with her.

"She had a thing for thugs and drug dealers," Bailey added.

"Was that because of her drug habit?" Carmen asked.

"No. Winter would always pay for what she got from them," Rosaland said and laughed. "That's why they liked her. Imagine being able to fuck your best customer."

"Any of these thugs and drug dealers capable of violence?"

"That would be Decatur Meriwether and Petre Gudaitis," Tomesia remarked.

Carmen glanced at her watch. "Thank you, ladies, for taking the time to speak to me about Winter, but I need to get back to the studio."

"I understand," Tomesia said and stood up to walk Carmen out of the restaurant.

As she headed back to the studio, Carmen made a call.

"This is Detective Mitchell."

"Hey, Diane, it's Carmen."

"I'm right in the middle of something. What do you need?"

"I'm gonna text you two names. Call me when you can," Carmen said and ended the call.

"Who was that?" her partner, Jack, asked.

"Carmen Taylor. She needs me to run some names for her," Diane said as they approached the door to Ryan Schlutz's apartment.

"You ready?" Jack said.

"As I'll ever be."

The detectives stepped to either side of the door and drew their weapons. Then Jack banged on the door.

"Ryan Schlutz, this is the police. We have a warrant for your arrest," Diane shouted.

Schlutz had kidnapped, raped, and brutally beaten a woman. She survived long enough to identify her attacker, whom she had met earlier that day when he came into the store where she worked.

The only thing she said to him was, "Have a nice day."

Schlutz was waiting for her when she came out of the store. She died two days later from her wounds, and Schlutz was charged with her murder.

Schlutz fired two shotgun blasts through the door. When there was a pause in the shooting, Jack quickly stepped in front of the door and kicked it in.

"Police!"

When Diane stepped into the unit, Schlutz was reloading the shotgun. Diane fired one shot that grazed Schlutz's shoulder, and he dropped the gun as he fell to the floor. While Diane covered him, Jack rushed up and kicked the shotgun away from Schlutz. He flipped him over and cuffed him.

"Ryan Schlutz, you're under arrest for the murder of Jewell Copeland. You have the right to remain silent. Anything you say can and will be used against you in a court of law. You have a right to an attorney."

Once the detectives got Schlutz back to the precinct, they booked and fingerprinted him. With that out of the way, Diane completed her paperwork before running the two names for Carmen.

"Carmen Taylor."

"Hey, Carmen, it's Diane. I was able to run those names for you."

"Thank you, Diane. What did you find out?"

"Both men are drug dealers with long records. What are you into?"

"I'm looking into the murderer of Patsy McWalter."

"That was about a year ago. Why the sudden interest?"

"I have a source providing me with new information."

"I'm assuming that you wanna talk to these jokers."

"You assume correctly."

"Well, Petre Gudaitis has been in prison for two and a half years."

"That eliminates him as a suspect."

"I have a last known address for Meriwether, but you are not going to talk to this asshole alone. Does Black still have a personal bodyguard for you?"

"I don't know. I know it ended when I moved to Atlanta and married Marcus. But now that I'm back, I don't know."

"Then you aren't going anywhere near him without me."

"Always glad for your company, Detective."

When Carmen and Diane arrived at the last known address of Decatur Meriwether, she knocked on the door. When Meriwether opened the door, he smiled at the sight of the two pretty women.

"What can I do for you ladies?"

"I'm Carmen Taylor with Channel 4 News. I'd like to ask you some questions about Patsy McWalter."

"You a cop?"

"No." She looked at him strangely and repeated herself. "I'm Carmen Taylor with Channel 4 News."

Meriwether pointed at Diane. “Who are you?”

“I’m the mean lady with the gun who is watching her back.”

“You’re the cop,” Meriwether said and stepped aside to allow them to enter. “What do you want?”

“I’d like to ask you some questions about Patsy McWalter.”

“Who?”

“Winter.”

Meriwether smiled at the mention of her name. “What you wanna know about the white girl?”

“Let’s start with the obvious question. Did you kill her?” Carmen asked.

“Oh, hell no. I did *not* kill the white girl.” He looked at Diane. “They tell me that killing white girls is bad on a nigga’s freedom.”

“When was the last time you spoke with her?” Carmen asked.

“It had been over a year before I heard she was dead. But I did see her at a party about a month before she died, but we didn’t speak.”

“Whose party was it? Do you remember?”

“Keith Stevens.”

“Now, you said that you hadn’t spoken to Winter in over a year before she was murdered.”

“That’s right.”

“So, you guys broke up?” Carmen asked.

“Yeah.”

“What happened?”

“She met a bigger fish.”

“Excuse me?”

“White girl had a thing for drugs, drug dealers, and the lifestyle. She couldn’t get enough of it.”

“The drugs or the lifestyle?”

"Both. The white girl could snort up Colombia, and she had the money to pay her own way. And she always wanted to be down."

"Can you think of anybody who would want to kill her?"

"Not for a fact. But the white girl could get on a nigga's last nerve sometimes, so I would look for whoever the new fish was before she died. Then I bet that you find your killer."

Chapter Thirteen

At nine o'clock, Carter went into Conversations to talk to Jackie about hitting Winston Townson. He walked through the club and took her private elevator upstairs to the third floor.

"Good evening, Mr. Garrison," Fiona said when Carter got out of the elevator.

"Evening, Fiona." He pointed to Jackie's office door. "She in?"

"Jackie is always in," she giggled and picked up the phone. "Mr. Garrison is here to see you."

"Please bring him in, Fiona," Jackie instructed.

Fiona ended the call and stood up. "Come with me, please, Mr. Garrison," she said, looping her arm in his. She escorted him into the office.

"What's up, Carter?" Jackie said as Fiona went to the bar in Jackie's office.

"How's it going tonight, Jackie?" Carter asked, and he took a seat in front of her desk.

"I'm having a good night tonight," she said as Fiona handed Carter a glass of Hennessy Paradis.

"Can I get anything for you, Jackie?"

"No, thank you, Fiona."

Fiona left the office.

"So, tell me, to what do I owe the honor?"

"I heard you have skills that I didn't know about."

Jackie laughed. "I have many skills that you don't know about. Which one are we talking about?"

"Mike tells me that you're a snipper."

Jackie laughed. "I can hit some shit from a distance. Since Black told you that, I assume you need that skill."

"I do."

"Who's the target?"

"Drug dealer named Winston Townson."

"Never heard of him. What did he do to get on your naughty list?"

"Mitch was selling drugs for him. Mitch is dead." Carter chuckled. "He 'sleeps with the fish.'"

"Townson had him killed?"

"I think so. Townson shows up at The Hole in the Wall, and a couple of hours later, his men toss a body in the trunk and dump him in the Hudson."

"That's fucked up."

"Tell me about it."

"The Hole in the Wall, that where these guys hang out?"

"They killed him there, so . . ."

"So, it's a safe bet that they run the joint." Jackie picked up her phone and made a call.

"'Sup, Boss?" Marvin answered.

"Come to my office."

"Be right there," he replied.

When he arrived at the office, Fiona offered him a drink.

"Chivas 12."

"I know what you drink, Money," Fiona said as she poured.

"You ever hear of a dope boy named Winston Townson?" Jackie asked when Fiona handed him his drink.

"Yeah, I've heard of him. He took over that crew when Modesto Colbert flipped on Akira Dennison and got her sent to prison."

"You or BC know where I can find him?"

"Yeah, they run their business out of a club called The Hole in the Wall."

"Thank you, Money."

"Anything me and BC can do for you?" Marvin asked.

"No, me and Carter got this, but I'll call if I need you."

"But you won't need help. You never do," Marvin replied as he finished his drink and stood up.

"True. I'll talk to you later." Jackie stood up. "Let's go."

"Right behind you," Carter said, standing and following Jackie out of her office. They got on the elevator, got into her car, and she drove them to The Hole in the Wall.

"I didn't know you were part of Colonel Mathis's team."

"An original member. It was me, Travis, Nick, Monika, and Xavier in those days. The Colonel had a lot of dirt on Travis for robbing banks and forced me to join the team to keep him out of jail."

Carter nodded his head and thought about it. "I would have thought Rain would be a part of that crew."

"She was, but the Colonel kicked her off the team."

"Why?"

"For saving Nick, X, and Monika's lives."

"Explain."

"She broke radio silence, thereby saving their lives. I will never forget that day." Jackie laughed. *"Jackie, we're in trouble. Drive the fuckin' truck through the fuckin' door,"* she said, imitating Rain's voice. "It's a good thing that I did come in when I did. Monika was shot, and Nick and the X-Man were pinned down. Rain saved the team that day, but the Colonel thought that she had a very volatile personality and would introduce an unstable element to the team."

Carter chuckled. "Rain? Volatile and unstable? Say it ain't so."

"Believe it or not." They rode in silence for a while. "So, what's up with you and Rain?"

"We're finding our way."

"I noticed that you said you talked to Mike."

"Yeah."

"That means you went around her, am I right?"

"You're right." Carter paused. "We might be working our way back, but I needed advice on what to do, not those fuckin' two-word answers she dishes out to me."

"I know. The shit can be frustrating, but she is the Boss of this Family."

"I know who she is, Jackie. You don't need to remind me."

"You two need to put this shit behind you and move forward. The shit y'all doing is bad for business."

"Yeah, Mike mentioned that too."

"So, after we take out this clown, you and me are going to Purple Rock for you to talk to Rain."

"Okay," Carter said as they arrived at The Hole in the Wall and went inside.

"You know what he looks like?" Jackie asked.

"I was hoping you knew him. You know everybody."

"Yeah, but not him." Jackie walked off, and Carter followed her to the bar. "Two shots of Hennessy XO."

"We got VSOP."

"Run it."

As the bartender went to make their drinks, they looked around the crowded club. When he returned with their drinks, Jackie peeled off a hundred-dollar bill and put it on the bar.

"Keep the change."

The bartender's eyes got big. "Thank you." When he reached for the bill, Carter put his hand on it.

"Winston Townson here tonight?" Jackie asked.

The bartender tugged lightly on the bill, and then he looked around the club.

He pointed. "That's him."

"The one in the fucked-up purple suit?" Jackie questioned.

"That's him," the bartender said, and Carter moved his hand.

Now that they had the information, the two shot their drinks and left the bar.

"You can't miss him in that purple suit," Carter said as they stepped outside.

"Tell me about it," Jackie replied.

She looked at the buildings around her for an excellent place to set up to take the shot. Once she had selected her spot, she went back to her car and opened the trunk. Carter was surprised that Jackie had an arsenal in her trunk that rivaled Rain's arsenal. She got her 308 Winchester Rifle and a couple of pairs of night vision goggles. She handed a pair to Carter, and he followed her into the building, where she had the best vantage point. When they reached the roof, Jackie set up her rifle, and Carter put on the night vision goggles.

"Now we wait," she said.

"I don't know how you do it," Carter commented after they had been there waiting for two hours, "staring into that scope for as long as you have." He shook his head. "I couldn't do it."

"It's not easy. You have to have patience, be disciplined, and rely on your training."

"Hold up. Purple suit coming out."

"I got him."

Jackie pulled the trigger and hit Townson with a headshot. As people panicked around him, his body fell to the ground. People frantically looked around for where the shot came from. With her task completed, Jackie packed up her rifle, and they returned to their car.

"Next stop, Purple Rock," Jackie said.

"Looking forward to it," Carter lied.

Going to Purple Rock to talk to Rain was the last thing he wanted to do. But Black all but ordered him to settle their differences. So, he would give it a shot, hoping Rain would be in a good mood that night.

Chapter Fourteen

"I can't find him."

"Let me make myself clear. If you don't find Jason Contreras, I'm gonna find you."

"Let me make some calls."

"Then I'll hear from you soon, right?"

"Right."

Rain ended the call and stood up. She holstered her weapons and went out onto the floor. It was another excellent night at Purple Rock. The house was packed. She sat down at her reserved table and looked at the stage. Cristal was up there performing a melody of her early hits. Despite RJ telling her that Cristal didn't play small venues like Purple Rock and that Gladys Gordan would object, it came about because Cristal liked Rain, and she wanted to play Purple Rock so much so that her one-night-only performance turned into an all-week performance.

A waitress approached Rain's table and placed a glass of Patrón on it.

"Can I get you anything else?"

"No, I'm good."

Rain took a sip as the waitress walked away. That was when she saw Carter come into her club, heading in her direction.

Fuck is he doing here?

Carter had never been to Purple Rock. He purposely avoided coming to any of Rain's clubs, and she was good with it. As he got closer, Rain saw Jackie trailing behind him. It made her feel a little better about his presence in her spot.

But still, what the fuck is he doing here? was the question that Rain asked herself.

"Hey, Rain," Jackie said and sat down. Carter stood in front of the table. Rain looked up at him.

"We need to talk."

"My office."

As Carter walked away from the table, Rain stood up and started for her office when she noticed that Jackie hadn't gotten up.

"Ain't you coming?" she asked as Carter walked away.

"Nope." Jackie shook her head. "This shit is between the two of you."

Rain gave Jackie the finger, rushed to catch up with Carter, and then led him to her office.

"What you wanna talk about?" Rain asked as soon as they were in her office, and the door closed.

"I wanted to say I'm sorry."

"For what?" Rain unholstered her guns.

"For everything that happened to us."

Rain shook her head. Like Carter, she had no interest in having this conversation. Still, she also knew that they needed to work out their differences, if only because Black had ordered them to do so, given the negative impact on business.

"Sit down, Carter."

Rain went behind her desk, and Carter sat down.

"You don't need to apologize. The shit was as much my fault as it was yours. More so if I want to be honest with you."

"I think we need some honesty between us."

"You're right, we do."

"What happened between you and me, Rain?"

"I decided that us fuckin' wasn't in the best interest of The Family." She paused. "I'm the Boss of this Family, and I need to stay objective. The way you were fuckin' me, I was losing that objectivity. And then I got pregnant."

"I understand," he may have said, but Carter didn't understand that shit at all. "What I don't understand is why you cut me off the way you did. I mean, one day, you're having the baby, and I wanna make it work; the next day, you tell me that you're having an abortion."

"You wanna know the reason why I cut you off?"

"Yes, Rain, I really wanna know," he said, paused, and decided to be totally honest with her. "I would love to know why you felt it necessary to cut me off the way you did, because, honestly, Rain, this shit had me fucked up for more than a minute."

Rain looked at Carter, and for the first time, she realized that he was hurt by it all. She thought that he simply shrugged it all off and moved on with his life.

"You wanna know why?"

"Yes, I really wanna know."

"Because I was catching for you, and you fucked Fantasy."

"Huh?"

Rain slammed her fist on the desk. "You *fucked* Fantasy!" she shouted.

"What?"

"You heard me, nigga."

"I haven't fucked Fantasy since before she went on her secret mission for Wanda."

Rain was surprised, and it showed on her face. "You didn't?" she questioned with her face contorted.

"No," Carter said adamantly.

"So, you're telling me that you didn't fuck her when you left the after-fight party at The Playhouse?"

"No." Carter paused and thought back to that night. "The rest of the team went back to Africa. She had monitor duty that night, so I drove her to the office."

"And you didn't fuck her?"

"No."

But in that moment, he wished he *had* fucked Fantasy that night. It wasn't like he didn't want to.

"If you thought I was fuckin' Fantasy, why didn't you just ask me?"

"I did, remember?" Rain said, and Carter looked at her curiously. "I said, 'When are you going to stop fuckin' around and tell me about Fantasy?' and when you didn't say anything, I hung up."

"I wish you hadn't hung up and let me explain." He shook his head in disgust. "But you know what? It probably wouldn't have mattered anyway."

"No, it wouldn't have mattered. Not at that point, anyway. I was too deep in my feelings by then." Rain paused. "I tried to tell myself that we were just fucking, and there was no need for discussion." She laughed. "And then I asked myself, if that was the case, why did it matter to me that you fucked her?"

"What did you come up with?"

"Because I was pregnant with your baby, nigga, *that's* why," she shouted as her phone rang. "This Rain."

"I got him."

"Where?"

When he told her where Jason Contreras could be found, she ended the call and looked at Carter. "Let's go. We got work to do."

Rain holstered her guns and left the office with Carter. They went to the table where Jackie was waiting.

"You two work it out?" Jackie asked as they passed the table.

"Let's go. We got work to do," Rain said and kept walking.

"Okay, guess not."

"We did," Rain said once they were outside the club.

"Good. That shit was bad for business. Now, where we going?"

"To kill somebody," Rain said, and Carter shrugged his shoulders as they made it to Rain's car.

When they arrived at the house where her snitch had told her Jason Contreras could be found, they got out of her car, and Rain opened her trunk. She took out her XRGL40 grenade launcher and two flash-bang smoke grenades with iron bots. She loaded the weapon, and they went toward the house. Rain fired twice.

Carter kicked in the door, and they rushed inside. Four men stood in the room, trying to breathe. Rain fired at them.

One of the men returned her fire, but she took aim and fired again. Her shot hit him in the back as he ran. Rain walked up to him and shot him twice more for good measure.

Jackie fired with both guns and hit her target with several shots to the chest. They split up. Carter heard a man coughing and went in after him. He walked up behind him and shot him in the back of the head.

Rain moved through the house, looking for Jason Contreras. When she saw him going up some steps, she followed him. When he reached the top of the stairs, he turned and fired at her. Rain slammed her back into the wall and returned his fire, running up the stairs two at a time, but when she reached the landing, he was nowhere in sight.

"Shit!"

She walked around the floor, looking for him. Rain went into a room and searched it, but saw that he wasn't hiding in there, so she exited the room and saw him heading for the stairs.

When he turned around, there was Rain with both of her guns pointed at him. Contreras raised his weapon.

"Time to die," she said and fired.

She rushed to the stairs and watched as Contreras tumbled down. Then she quickly came down the stairs where Jackie and Carter were standing, awaiting her.

"Everything all right?" Jackie asked.

Then Rain shot Contreras twice in the head.

"Now it is," she replied and holstered her weapon.

"I think he was already dead," Carter said as he and Jackie followed Rain out of the house.

"I think so too," Jackie said.

"Just making sure," Rain replied, and they got into her car.

"Are we done for the night, or do we got some more bodies to drop?" Jackie asked.

"Yeah. We're done for the night," Rain said as they drove off.

"Drop me off at the club," Jackie requested.

When they reached Conversations, she got out, and Rain drove back to Purple Rock.

"We good?" Carter asked as she drove.

"Yeah, we're good. And I'll try not to go outta my way to be an asshole."

"I'm good with that." They drove in silence for a while. "There's something I need to make you aware of. Something I should have come to you with."

"But you didn't because you were into your feelings." She smiled. It was good to see her smiling again. It had been so long since he'd seen it.

"Yeah." Carter paused because she was right. "One of our dancers, Vixen. She dances at Envy."

"I know Vixen, go on."

"Carmen Taylor got her into modeling, and she was doing a fashion show in Nassau."

"Nassau? Is Jada West involved in this?"

"Not to my knowledge, but I got Carmen and Mercedes looking into that for me."

"She's in New York. You could have asked her yourself. One more reason why you could have come to me with this."

"Point taken."

"Good for you. Now, you're learning," Rain said playfully. If she wanted to be honest, there were times when she missed being with him.

"Mitch was down there."

"Where? In Nassau?"

"Yes."

"What the fuck was he doing there?"

"I don't know what he was up to, but there was a shooting at the show."

Rain shook her head. "Was Mitch involved in the shooting?"

"Vixen didn't know. She didn't see it go down. I had someone follow Mitch to a bar owned by Winston Townson. My guy can't say for sure, but they dumped what looked like a body into the Hudson River."

"Damn. Even though he was dealing, Mitch was still a member of this Family. We can't let that go unanswered." Rain paused and thought for a second. Her eyes narrowed. "You went around me and talked to Black about this, didn't you?"

"Yeah. Since we don't wanna go to war over a guy we were gonna kill anyway, and Monika is out of the country, Mike suggested that I use Jackie."

"She's good with a rifle."

"She hit him outside his spot tonight."

Rain paused and shook her head. "This can't happen no more. I can't have you doing end-arounds on me. That shit is bad for business."

"So everybody keeps telling me. The captain needs to get along with the boss of his Family."

Rain pointed at Carter's face. "And *that's* why I never should fucked you in the first place, and that's on me." She got out, slammed the door, and walked back into the club.

"Well, that went well."

Chapter Fifteen

After leaving Rain at Purple Rock, Carter drove to Knuckles's gambling spot. When he walked in, the first person he noticed was Crimson. Knowing that she danced with a partner at Shooters, he looked around for Sizzle. Once he spotted her, he looked around for Knuckles's wife, Kelsey. She was sitting in her usual spot at a table where she could see the entire room. Carter angrily headed in that direction.

"Hey, Skipper," Kelsey said, smiling her bright, beautiful smile.

She was a beautiful woman with auburn skin and long, flowing, skinny braids that hung down her back. Her chiseled facial features, angular nose, and jawline accented her eyes.

That night, Kelsey was dressed elegantly in a Marchesa Notte cloqué gown that featured a one-shoulder ruffle with a sweetheart neckline and a gathered design on the skirt that exposed her left leg. She began wearing gowns the night she visited La Chat and saw how Mercedes dressed.

When she asked why she wore gowns, Mercedes informed her that, "This is how a lady dresses," she smiled. "This is how Jada West taught me a lady who runs an upscale Mike Black establishment dresses."

Even though she wasn't trained by nor had she ever met the great Jada West, Kelsey had heard wonderful things about her. And it occurred to her that she, like Mercedes, ran an upscale Mike Black club, or at the very least, she wanted her spot to be considered upscale, so she began dressing the part. And then it occurred to her that to be regarded as an upscale spot, she needed upscale women working the floor, which prompted the recruiting push.

"Evening, Kelsey. Mind if I sit?"

"Not at all."

"Thank you." Carter sat down and spotted Crimson and Sizzle. He pointed. "How long have they been working here?"

"It's not what you think." Kelsey put her hands up in surrender. "I talked to them about making the move to work here weeks ago. They just recently decided to do it. So, yes, Carter, this is their first night on the floor. So, no, Skipper, I have not defied your orders."

"Don't get me wrong. I want you to have the best women working here."

"So do I."

"But there are plenty of other clubs you can recruit from that we don't own."

"I understand."

"Make sure." Carter pointed at her face. "So I'll tell you what's gonna happen now. You're gonna talk to Horne, and you are going to compensate him for the loss of his two top earners." He pointed at her face again. "Are we clear, Kelsey?"

"Crystal clear, Skipper."

"I'm glad you finally understand me."

"I do."

"Good. We are just getting to the point where a better quality of dancers is coming back after the serial killer terrorized our spots."

"It was one of my best recruiting features."

"How's that?"

"Everybody in here has been checked out and vetted. So, the ladies would feel safe working here."

Carter nodded. "I take it that you know who all these people are?"

"I do. There may be a few that I couldn't call out off the top of my head, but yeah, I know who's in my joint."

Carter nodded and looked around for somebody that he didn't know.

"Who's that guy?" he pointed. "The one in the light blue suit."

"His name is Cole Thompson. We call him 'Colors,' because he always wears something colorful. He manages a hedge fund. In addition to liking to lose at poker, he likes to bet on the ponies."

Carter looked around again, and that was when he saw her. "Who's that?"

Kelsey smiled. "I was wondering if you were going to notice her."

"How could I *not* notice her. She's beautiful."

"That she is. Her name is Gianna Matisse. She came with Kamari Andrews a couple of weeks ago, and she's been coming here without him ever since."

"What do you know about her?"

"That her money is good mostly."

"What does that mean?"

"That I checked her out, and I can't find anything on her past two or three years."

"You think she's a cop?"

"No. If she were a cop, her background would be pristine, and it would go back to her childhood." Kelsey shook her head. "No. It's more like she paid for that identity, but it wasn't fully formed. But like I said, her money is good. But here's the thing about Ms. Gianna Matisse. It's like she just likes to gamble. She doesn't win big, doesn't lose big; she maintains."

"Interesting."

"I thought so, but like I said, her money's been good."

"I'll have my people do a deep dive into her. Now, where's Knuckles?"

"In the office."

"He alone?" Carter asked and stood up.

"Far as I know."

"I know how he likes to sample the new merchandise."

"If that were going on, I would be in there with him," she shouted as Carter walked away.

After talking to Knuckles in the office, Carter came out and saw that Gianna Matisse was playing roulette.

"Who's that?" he asked Knuckles.

"Her name is Gianna Matisse. She came with Kamari Andrews several weeks ago. She's been coming here without him ever since. Kelsey checked her out and—" Knuckles said and signed for Kelsey to join him.

"No need." Carter held up his hand. "She told me about her being a ghost before three years ago. I'll have my people check her out," he said, all but staring at her.

And then she stood up. Carter was speechless as she turned toward him, wearing a red sleeveless Akris V-neck sheath dress with a plunging V-neckline and side slits. His eyes blazed a trail down her legs to her feet, which were adorned with Jimmy Choo satin sandals.

They made eye contact. Gianna smiled at him, and Carter smiled back. He continued watching as she asked the dealer to have someone take her chips to the cash room to get paid. Then she tossed a hundred-dollar chip onto the table, and the dealer signaled for Security to escort her.

"See to it that Ms. Matisse makes it safely to the cash register room."

Security looked at Gianna, and once he smiled, he picked up her chips. "Right this way, Ms. Matisse."

Carter continued to watch as Kelsey joined them at the bar.

"What's up, babe?"

"Carter wants to know about Gianna Matisse."

Kelsey looked at the spot until she spotted her, then turned to Carter, noticing how he was watching her.

"What else do you want to know about her, Skipper?"

"Everything. Like who she was before three years ago. Something about that bothers me."

"I'm on it, Skipper. You can count on that."

Carter made no secret of the fact that he was watching her as the security guard escorted her to the cage to cash in her chips. While she waited for her money, she glanced in Carter's direction and saw how he was watching her. She nodded to acknowledge him. Carter nodded at her. Once she had her money, Security escorted her to the exit, and Carter watched her leave.

He was about to go after Gianna Matisse when she walked out, but that was when Vixen walked in. Thinking that Kelsey had recruited her to work there, he immediately got mad and approached her.

"What are you doing here?"

"I'm looking for you."

"Me?" Carter pointed to himself.

"Yes, you, Mr. Garrison. I know you're usually here making the rounds, so here I am."

"Well, here I am. What can I do for you?"

"I came to thank you."

"For what?"

"I got a call today from Erykah Morgan at Prestige Capital and Associates about a job. I was so excited that I called Carmen to thank her, and she said that it wasn't her. She said that she mentioned it to you, and you probably arranged it. So, I came to say thank you."

"No worries. Just do a good job, and don't let me down."

"I promise that I won't."

"You know what you'll be doing?"

"She said that I would be part of the intern program."

"Well, good luck. I'm sure you'll be fine."

It was then that a man came to the club. Since nobody had seen him in there before, Knuckles and Security approached him.

"What can I do for you?" Knuckles asked.

"I'm looking for Mitchell Wright. I heard he hangs out here."

"Who are you?"

"A friend," the man said, but that was when he spotted Vixen.

Therefore, when Security moved closer to him, the man went for his gun. However, Knuckles already had his gun out and shot the man twice in the head, killing him instantly.

"Who was that?" Carter asked.

"I don't know. He said he was a friend of Mitch, but when we started to move in, he went for his gun."

"The question is why," Carter said.

"No idea."

"Maybe you should have asked before you killed him," Carter said.

Knuckles shrugged his shoulders. "Maybe."

Chapter Sixteen

"Good morning, and welcome to Prestige Capital and Associates. How may I help you today?" Vandy asked the following morning.

"I'm Victoria Howard. I have an interview with Erykah Morgan."

Vandy looked up at the woman who was conservatively dressed in a tie-front sheath dress that screamed, "I am *not* a dancer at Club Envy." She thought that this woman must be somebody because Erykah never personally interviewed anybody.

"If you wouldn't mind having a seat, I will let Ms. Morgan know that you're here."

"Thank you."

When she turned to go sit down, Vandy dialed Erykah's extension.

"Erykah Morgan."

"It's Vandy. I have a Victoria Howard in the lobby to see you."

"I'll be out in a minute."

When Erykah arrived in the lobby, Vandy pointed her out, and she approached Vixen.

"Good morning. My name is Erykah Morgan. How are you doing today?"

Vixen stood up. "I am doing great."

"Good. If you'll follow me, we'll get started."

It wasn't much of an interview. Erykah asked her some basic questions as she took her on a tour of the office, introducing her to several department heads along the way.

When they arrived at the Entertainment Division, Erykah stopped at the door and turned to Vixen.

"You're being hired into our intern program," Erykah began and told Vixen what her salary would be. "I have to insist that you not discuss your salary with any of the other interns."

"Yes, ma'am."

"My name is Erykah or Ms. Morgan." She smiled. "If you call me ma'am again, you're fired."

Vixen giggled, but Erykah didn't. She reached for the doorknob and went into the Entertainment Division.

"You're being assigned to the Entertainment Division," she said as she entered Gladys Gordon's office. "Good morning, Gladys."

"Good morning, Erykah."

"I'd like to introduce you to your new intern, Victoria Howard."

Gladys stood up, came from behind her desk, and shook Vixen's hand. "Good to meet you, Victoria."

"I'll leave you in Gladys's capable hands," Erykah said and left the office.

Gladys took Vixen around, introducing her to the department heads and some of the key people in the division.

"And this is your office," Gladys said, ushering her into the room.

"What will I be doing?"

"Right now, your job is to answer the phone and do whatever needs doing around here, and we'll see where you fit in once I see what kind of skills you have."

Vixen sat down at her desk. "And how do you want me to answer the phone?"

"Entertainment Division, this is Victoria. How should I direct your call?" Gladys said as the phone rang. Vixen answered.

"Entertainment Division, this is Victoria. How should I direct your call?" Vixen said, and Gladys handed her the phone directory and left the office.

That night, Vixen went to Club Envy to resign.

"Congratulations. What will you be doing?" the manager, Vanessa Jennings, asked.

"Answering the phone and doing whatever needs doing," she giggled. "I'm basically the office flunky."

"Well, congratulations."

"Thank you."

"But I need a favor."

"What's that?"

"Kelsey's been up to her old tricks."

"Again?"

"Yes, again. So, I'm short on dancers tonight. Would you mind staying and dancing this one last time?"

"Not at all. I'll go get changed."

"Thank you, Vixen," Vanessa said, and Vixen headed toward the dressing room, cursing herself for coming to quit in person. She could have done without the few outfits she had there and would be perfectly content never to set foot in a place like that ever again. But she felt like she owed that to Vanessa.

As she undressed, Vixen reflected on the opportunity before her and how grateful she was to be standing there. It was as if everything had fallen into place perfectly. From the chance meeting with Carmen to Carter hooking her up with a job, what more could she ask for?

"Not to be here," she said aloud and laughed. She put on her favorite outfit. A hot pink bustier and thong set. When she came out on the floor, Vixen took a look at the packed house of men with fists full of money and decided that she would dance when it was her time on stage, but that would be all. No table dancing for her; she was done with this part of her life. She looked around and hoped to see one of her regulars. That way, she could sit all night and not really have to be bothered.

"Otis. Good," she said and headed straight for him. He smiled when he saw her coming. "Hey, Otis."

"How are you tonight, Vixen?"

"A little tired," she said and sat down. And for her, that was going to be it for the night.

Her plan was working. Vixen had been there for an hour, and she hadn't moved out of her chair.

"Vixen. You're up next," the DJ announced, letting her know that after that three-song set, he would be calling her to the main stage to dance.

A few minutes later, Telvin Henderson and James Bellamy came into Club Envy and sat at a table. They were the two men who killed Mitch. Henderson flagged down a waitress.

"Bring us a pitcher of beer and a couple of shots of Jose 1800," Henderson ordered.

"And send some hoes over here," Bellamy shouted. He was drunk off his ass already and planned to get shit-faced and would be carried out.

The waitress sent over three women to dance and went to get their drinks. Henderson pulled out a roll of bills. All three quickly got naked and went to work.

"Coming to the main stage, Vixen," the DJ announced, and she got up and began making her way forward.

She had gotten through the first two up-tempo songs and had settled into a slow, seductive groove, crawling on stage to get some money . . . when she saw them. Vixen recognized them right away and froze. Hoping that they didn't see her, she stood up and tried to finish her set without looking in that direction. But it was too late.

Henderson tapped Bellamy. “What?” he shouted angrily because the dancer had her titties in his face.

“Ain’t that the bitch that was in Nassau with Mitch?” Henderson asked, and Bellamy pushed the dancer out of the way.

“Asshole!” she shouted, grabbed her clothes, and walked away. The other two kept dancing.

“That’s her. You think she saw us?”

“Does it matter?”

“What you wanna do?”

“We need to take care of her,” Henderson said.

“No shit. What you wanna do?”

“When she gets done on stage, we take her,” Henderson said as the last song of her set ended, and Vixen began gathering up the money on the stage. They stood up and approached the stage, but before they could get to her, Vixen jumped off it and rushed to the dressing room. Henderson and Bellamy moved to catch up with her, but they were too slow, and Security stopped them.

“Fuck you niggas think you’re going? You can’t go back there,” the security guard said, and they backed off.

“What now?”

“We wait,” Henderson said, and they went to sit down at a nearby table.

When Vixen got into the dressing room, tears of fear were streaming down her cheeks.

“What’s wrong?” Vanessa asked.

“The men I saw in Nassau with Mitch are here.”

“In the club?”

“Yes,” she cried.

“Show me,” Vanessa demanded, and she followed Vixen to the door. She pointed them out. “Don’t worry. You stay in here, and I’ll handle them.” Vanessa took out her phone.

“Hey, Vanessa. What’s up?” Angel asked.

"Where are you?"

"Out riding with Bowie. What's up?"

"The men that Vixen saw in Nassau are here, and they're after her."

"We're on our way," Angel said and ended the call.

"What's up?" Bowie asked.

"The men that Vixen saw in Nassau are at Envy," Angel informed him, and Bowie drove in that direction.

Henderson and Bellamy were still sitting at the table, waiting for Vixen to come out of the dressing room, when Angel and Bowie arrived. Vanessa pointed them out, and they approached the table.

"Time for you gentlemen to leave," Angel said.

"Who the fuck are you?" Bellamy asked.

"I'm the bitch that just told you to get the fuck outta here." Angel took out two Berettas. "And I ain't gonna tell you again."

Henderson wisely put up his hands and slowly stood up. Bellamy wasn't as smart. He bounced out of his chair and lunged at Angel. Bowie stepped up quickly and punched him in the face. He dropped like a rock.

Bowie waved Security over, and they picked up Bellamy and carried him out the back door. With Angel's guns in his back, Henderson walked out behind them. When they were outside, Security dropped Bellamy and went back inside.

Angel kicked Bellamy. "Get up!" She kicked him again. "I said, 'Get up,' muthafucka."

This time, Bellamy rose to his feet and stood beside Henderson. Angel raised her weapons and shot them both in the chest. Once they fell to the ground, she shot them in the head.

"Call Edwina," Angel said, and Bowie took out his phone.

Chapter Seventeen

Romans, the pizzeria and sports bar controlled by Carter Garrison's crew, was that evening's destination for Kelsey Nelson. She had come there looking for Carter to tell him what she'd had, or, more correctly, *hadn't* learned about Gianna Matisse. She found Carter's interest in the beauty interesting, to say the least. It made her wonder if he was interested in her for security reasons or personal ones. Although Kelsey was married to Knuckles and she loved him, she'd always thought her captain was one fine-ass man. One that she'd be willing to try if he showed her any attention.

Which he hadn't. But a woman can dream.

When Kelsey arrived at Romans, she went to the counter.

"What can I get for you, Kelsey?"

"Is the Skipper here?"

"He's in his office."

"Thanks," she said and began making her way through the crowd of sports gamblers to the office. She knocked on the door.

"Come!"

Kelsey entered the office and found Carter sitting behind his desk.

That is one fine-ass man, she thought, looking at Carter, who was dressed in a midnight-blue, tailored-fit Havana suit.

"Hey, Skipper."

"What's up, Kelsey?" Carter asked and was a little surprised to see her there. "What brings you here?"

"I came to see you."

"Really?"

"Yes, really," Kelsey said, sitting in front of his desk.

"And why is that?"

"You told me you wanted me to look into Gianna Matisse."

Kelsey smiled when Carter sat up a little straighter.

"What did you find out?"

"What I found out is that Gianna Matisse is a ghost."

"What does that mean?"

"Near as I can tell, before a year or two ago, Gianna Matisse didn't exist."

"Thanks," he said, but he was intrigued.

Kelsey was surprised by his reaction. However, it confirmed her suspicion that his interest in Gianna Matisse was personal. It gave her hope that she might have a chance.

"Anything else you need me to do for you, Skipper?"

"Yeah." Carter paused. "Discreetly get a picture of her." He held up one finger. "Discreetly, Kelsey. Ghosts tend to be camera shy."

Kelsey saluted and stood up. "Understood, Skipper."

With that, Kelsey returned to Knuckles's gambling spot. When she arrived, she looked around until she spotted her. That night, the lovely Ms. Matisse was wearing a black Saint Laurent wrap dress and Dune slingback pumps. As she usually did, Gianna was holding her own at the poker table, neither winning nor losing. It was as if she were playing because she enjoyed the game rather than trying to make money.

As discreetly as possible, Kelsey took a picture of Gianna Matisse and sent it to Carter.

"Thanks."

The following day, Carter made a rare appearance at Nick's office. Although he knew about their capabilities, he had never had a need to utilize them before. Since he had only been there once, Carla was shocked to look up and see him coming through the door.

"No, that is *not* Carter Garrison," she said.

"Yes, it is," Carter replied, coming into the office. "How are you doing, Carla?"

"No, that *ain't* Carter Garrison I hear in my office," said a loud, booming voice.

Carter spun around at the sound of the familiar voice. "Nick."

Nick came out of his office and shook hands with Carter. "How's it going?"

"Doing great," Carter said.

"Wondering what it took to get an old-school leg breaker like you to come to the land of high-tech dreams."

"I need to run facial recognition on somebody," Carter said.

"Wow," Carla replied.

He handed the image that Kelsey had captured to Carla. Nick leaned in and glanced at the picture.

"She's pretty, Carter. Who is she?" he asked.

"Her name is Gianna Matisse. She came to Knuckles's joint several weeks ago with Kamari Andrews. Been going there ever since."

"I know Kelsey checks out all of their clients," Carla said, running her facial recognition on the image.

"She did, and she said that before two or three years ago, Gianna Matisse didn't exist."

"You think she's a cop?" Nick asked as Carla proceeded with her task.

"Kelsey doesn't think so. She said if she were a cop, the identity would be more detailed and flawless."

"That's true," Carla stated. "If she were a cop, they would have dotted every i and crossed every t."

"Kelsey said that this identity seems incomplete."

"I agree," Carla concurred.

"I see why that would be concerning to you." Nick leaned closer to Carter. "It wouldn't have anything to do with the fact that she's beautiful, would it?"

"No." Carter laughed. "At this point, my interest in her is purely professional. Not knowing who she really is and what she's doing in my joint represents a threat."

"Right. At this point," Nick laughed. "I didn't just meet you, brother. Me and you go back to the old days."

"So, you know this is strictly business."

"Until it's not."

"Right."

"I got you, Carter," Carla said. "Give me a day or two, and I'll tell you everything there is to know about Gianna Matisse."

"Thanks, Carla." He turned to Nick and shook his hand. "Good seeing you, Nick."

"What are you getting ready to do now?" Nick asked as they started for the door.

"Nothing. Why?"

"Have a drink with me."

"I tell you what. Come on to Romans with me. I'll buy you a drink, *and* I'll get you a slice."

"Sounds good. I'm gone for the night, Carla," Nick said.

"Good night, gentlemen," she replied.

"How's married life treating you?" Carter asked.

"It is what it is," Nick said, and they left the office.

The following day, Carla called Carter and asked him to come to the office to discuss Gianna Matisse.

"Give me a couple of hours."

When he arrived, Carla told him that she had run facial recognition on the image and conducted a deep dive on Gianna Matisse.

"Kelsey was right. Before two years ago, Gianna Matisse didn't exist."

"Thanks, Carla," he said, but he was even more intrigued now.

"Do you want me to dig deeper?"

"No. I mean, if something just jumps out at you, but no."

"I'm gonna keep digging," she promised. "Something about her doesn't seem right to me."

"I get that feeling too. Let me know if you find out anything," he said and headed for the elevator.

"Will do."

Later that night, Carter went to Knuckles's spot. Gianna Matisse was there, playing poker as usual.

"What did you find out?" Knuckles asked.

"About?"

Knuckles discreetly pointed at Gianna. "About our friend there."

"Carla couldn't get anything on her either."

"That's not good." Knuckles paused. "But it ain't necessarily bad either."

Carter looked strangely at Knuckles. "How you figure?" he asked.

"If she were a cop, Kelsey would have sniffed her out, and Carla would definitely know it."

"True. But who is she, and what is she doing here? *That's* the question."

Carter looked at Gianna Matisse, and all he could think of at that moment was how incredibly beautiful she was. Her lips seemed to be speaking his name. Her soft, dark eyes invited him in. Her high cheekbones made her jawline, often considered a sign of femininity and grace, look more defined in the dimly lit room.

And then she looked up, and their eyes connected for the first time that night. Gianna smiled at Carter, and he nodded his head to acknowledge her. Now, he couldn't stop looking at her and had to force himself to look away. But he couldn't. He stood spellbound as Gianna gathered her chips.

"Well, boys, I think I've taken enough of your money for one night." She stood up. "I think I'll try my luck at the roulette table," she said, looking at Carter.

That evening, Gianna was wearing a sleeveless Erdem pencil midi-dress. Her feet were adorned in Christian Louboutin metallic leather mules, and she carried a Christian Louboutin clutch.

Gianna went to the roulette table and sat down.

"Place your bets."

Her bet was $5,000 on thirty-two red.

Should he try to talk to her, or should he continue to stand and stare at her?

He chose the latter.

Carter stood and watched her as the wheel spun. At thirty-five to one odds on a $5,000 bet, her winning could cost him a chunk of cash.

"Twenty-four black."

Carter exhaled.

He watched as she got up from the roulette table, gathered her remaining chips, and asked to be escorted to the cage so she could cash out for the evening. Carter tapped Knuckles, and he went to escort Gianna Matisse out of the spot.

"Enjoy the rest of your evening," Knuckles said.

"Thank you," she replied and looked back at Carter.

He picked up his glass, and she winked at him before she left the spot.

Chapter Eighteen

"Do you know what I did with my bikini, Michael?" Shy shouted from her closet.

"No," he shouted back.

"I know I took it out. Where could it be?"

"Did you look in your suitcase?"

"What are you trying to say?" Shy asked, coming out of the closet.

"That you might have already packed it. If not, you can always get one when you get there."

"I might even have one that still fits me at the house," Shy said, thinking that it had been awhile since she'd been to their home in Freeport. She looked in the suitcase. "Here it is."

"Told you." He thought of a question. "Why am I packed and you're not?"

"Because you are easy to pack for. You don't care how you look."

"Nope. I just wanna be with you."

"And I just wanna be with you. I just wanna look good doing it, though."

"And I *do* care. Kinda." He paused. "And besides, whatever we forget, we can get while we're there. So, it's no big deal to me."

"I know, but I thought that the point of going to Freeport instead of someplace else is that I won't want or need to do any shopping." Shy paused.

"Unless, of course, you want me to go shopping."

"No, I most certainly do *not* want you to go shopping."

"It's our house. You know that you can go nude if you want to."

"I could, but I'm not," Shy giggled. "Maybe we could go skinny dipping in our pool late at night."

"*That's* what I'm talking about."

"I know. But I promise you, Cassandra Black will not be seen naked on the beach. Not gonna happen—ever."

"You would draw a crowd."

"And seriously, Michael, is that *really* what you want?"

"Nope. But the idea of us, naked and fuckin' in the pool by the moonlight, does sound like something we should do nightly."

"I'll think about it," Shy said and went to finish packing for their trip to Freeport.

After that, Black took the suitcases downstairs, where their family had gathered to see them off. As Chuck and William took the luggage to the car, Shy walked up to Eazy and put her hands on his shoulders.

"I need you to behave yourself and do what your grandmothers and your sister say. Do you understand me, young man?"

"Yes, Mommy."

Shy shook her head. "Don't just 'Yes, Mommy' me, Eazy."

"I'm not."

"Good. Because you know I will drop what I'm doing and make Jake fly me back here. And that will *not* go well for you. Do you understand?"

"Yes, Mommy. I mean, I understand," Eazy said and hugged his mother.

Michelle stepped up and hugged her parents.

"I'm depending on you to keep things in order here," Shy told her daughter.

"I know. And I got it, Mommy," Michelle said confidently. "You don't have to worry about that. You don't have anything to worry about." She looked at the brother. "Ain't that right, Eazy?"

"Right. You two have a good time because there's nothing for you to worry about here."

"You two enjoy yourselves, and don't worry about us," Michelle said.

Black looked at Michelle.

"I'll call you when we get to Nassau," Black said, and Shy looked at him because she thought that the plan was to go to Freeport. She read his eyes. "You call Rain and tell her where we are, and then you call Bobby and let him know too."

"I will. Do you want me to call Aunt Wanda and let her know too?"

"Yeah," Black nodded.

"You two have a good time."

"We will," Shy said.

Black and Shy left the house, and William drove them away. She moved close to him and whispered.

"I thought we were going to Freeport," she questioned.

He took her hand in his and kissed it. Black smiled. "We are."

"Okay. Then . . ."

He took her hand to his lips and kissed it again.

"What is the best way to be alone in Freeport?" he asked and looked into his wife's eyes.

Shy thought for a second or two. "If everyone thinks we're in Nassau."

"See?" Black squeezed her hand. "I knew you were more than just a pretty face."

"I try to be," Shy said and settled in for the ride to the airport.

So, William drove them to the airport. Jake filed a flight plan to Nassau, and once William loaded their luggage, they boarded the jet.

"How long are you going to stay in Nassau, Boss?" William asked.

"A few days."

"Have a safe flight and a good time."

"Thank you, William, we will," Shy said, and he got off the jet.

"You wanna take us up, Mrs. Black?" Jake asked.

"It's been a minute since I've flown."

Shy thought about it. This Cessna was new, so she hadn't piloted it since Black and Jake bought it.

"Sure, why not?" Shy said and followed Jake to the cockpit. As Shy took a seat and put on some headphones, Black sat down and fastened his seat belt.

"Good morning, Tower. This is Lima-Yankee-Foxtrot-Tango requesting ATC clearance."

"Good morning, Lima-Yankee-Foxtrot-Tango. You are cleared to destination Nassau via the flight planned route."

Shy taxied the aircraft into position. Once there, she contacted the tower.

"Lima-Yankee-Foxtrot-Tango, requesting start-up."

"Lima-Yankee-Foxtrot-Tango, start-up approved. Runway is in use seven."

Shy piloted the Cessna to runway seven and requested clearance from the tower to proceed.

"Lima-Yankee-Foxtrot-Tango requesting taxi."

"Lima-Yankee-Foxtrot-Tango, you are cleared to taxi to holding point runway seven."

Upon reaching runway seven, she informed the tower she was ready for departure and waited for the clearance signal.

"Take us up," Jake said.

"Here we go," Shy said and moved the throttle forward to increase power.

She used the rudder pedals to steer the airplane's nosewheel onto the runway centerline to align the aircraft and nosewheel with the runway. After releasing the brakes, Shy advanced the throttle smoothly and continued to takeoff power. Once she had reached a cruising altitude of 35,000 feet, she turned the controls over to Jake.

"Great job, Mrs. Black," he said.

"Thank you, Jake," she replied before leaving the cockpit.

"Smooth takeoff," Black said when Shy came out of the cockpit. He unbuckled his seat belt and got up.

"Thank you." Shy went to the bar. "You want a drink?"

"I was just about to ask you the same question," he said and sat down. "I would love a drink, my love. Thank you."

Once Shy had poured Black a glass of Louis XIII and a Don Q Gran Añejo for herself, she took a seat, handing him his drink.

"Thank you."

"Does Jake know?" Shy asked.

"Does Jake know what? Where we're really staying?"

"Yes."

"Yes, he does. He has to come get us when we're ready to come home." She giggled. "So, Mr. Black, where are we staying in Nassau?"

"The Island House," he said, and handed Shy the brochure.

"Luxury hotel with a boutique vibe. Just thirty rooms. I like that." Shy read further and sipped her drink. "Separate soaking tubs and rain showers. Lap pool, you should like that, a twenty-four-hour gym, and squash courts." Shy looked up from the brochure. "What is squash?"

"I have no idea."

"It's got a spa on the property," Shy said, continuing to read from the brochure. "They have Italian and Southeast Asian restaurants on the property, and they have wine tastings." She closed the brochure and handed it to Black. "Next time we have to go to Nassau, we should stay there."

"It does sound nice, doesn't it?"

"It does."

Upon arrival at Lynden Pindling International Airport, Jake took care of the luggage while Mr. and Mrs. Black took a limousine to The Island House and checked into a suite.

"What now?" Shy asked.

"Are you hungry?"

"How long have you known me?"

"Long enough to know that you're always hungry. Let's go eat," Black said, and the limousine took them to Tuga Supper Club in the Lyford Cay Marina.

After dining on rib steak fries and lobster tails, Black and Shy left the Tuga Supper Club, and once again, Shy asked, "What now?"

"You know, you ask a lot of questions. Questions, questions, always questions, with you," he said, taking her hand.

"Yes. Like you said, I'm more than just a pretty face, so I ask questions. Mommy used to say that fools ask questions to be made wise," Shy said, and they walked hand in hand past boats, big and small.

"I've heard her say that to you," he chuckled. "Michelle and Eazy too."

"It is one of her standards."

They kept walking along the dock until they reached a boat that Shy recognized.

"Permission to come aboard," Black shouted, and Oscar appeared on the deck of the ship.

"Permission granted," he shouted back.

"Smart."

"Yeah, I'm more than just a pretty face too," Black said and escorted Shy aboard the ship that they owned, and Jada had been using to shuttle her clients from Nassau to Freeport.

"Good afternoon, Mrs. Black," Oscar said.

"How have you been, Oscar?"

"I've been doing fine, Mrs. Black. What about you?"

"I'm absolutely wonderful. Excited to be here."

"I'm glad to have you sailing with me again."

"Are we ready to shove off?" Black asked.

"Whenever the word is given."

"The word is given. Set sail for Freeport," Black said.

Oscar saluted, and they set sail for Freeport. Black put his arms around Shy.

"In a few hours, we'll be in Freeport." He nuzzled her neck. "All alone for as long as you can stand me."

"I like that."

Chapter Nineteen

After checking in with Horne at Shooters, Carter left there on his way to Club Envy. When he arrived, the house was on edge, still reeling from the events of the last evening when men tried to take Vixen by force. Vanessa had kept what was going on with Vixen and Mitch away from the other dancers, who were just starting to feel comfortable after the serial killer scare.

It was Angel and Bowie who had taken care of the killer, so their appearance at Club Envy to deal with Bellamy and Henderson was unsettling for the women who just wanted a safe place to work.

"How's it going tonight?" Carter asked.

"We got a good crowd, niggas spending that money," Vanessa reported.

"What happened last night?"

"I was in the dressing room when Vixen came back there crying. When I asked her what was wrong, she said that the men that she saw in Nassau with Mitch were in the house."

"What did they want?"

"I didn't ask, but I'm guessing that they wanted her," Vanessa said, stating the obvious.

"You think they came here looking for her, or did they just show up here and recognize her from Nassau?"

"I can't say for sure. Angel and Bowie don't ask no questions, but I don't think so."

"Why don't you think they came here looking for her?"

"Because I saw them when they came in. One of them was drunk off his ass when he got here. You don't get fucked up like he was and have to put in work." Vanessa shook her head. "No, Carter, I believe it was random."

"How did Angel and Bowie leave it?"

Vanessa leaned closer to Carter. "Dead." She stepped back. "You know how they do it. They called Edwina, and she did her thing."

Carter chuckled. "They keep Edwina busy."

"They most certainly do."

"Where's Vixen?"

"Last night was her last night working. Said you hooked her up with a job at Prestige Capital and Associates. Today was her first day at work." Vanessa paused. "And I'll thank you not to hook up any of my other dancers. Bad enough I got Kelsey to deal with. I don't need you poaching any more of my dancers too."

"Kelsey hasn't been here in the last few days, has she?" Carter wanted to know.

"I haven't seen her, and she usually shows up here at least twice a week."

"If she shows her face in here, I wanna know about it. Understand?"

"Understood."

"I'm going to get a drink, and then I'm outta here," Carter said, walking away from Vanessa.

As he went to the bar, the bartender saw him coming and had a glass of Hennessy Paradis waiting for him.

"Thanks." Carter shot the drink and left Club Envy.

His next stop was La Chat to check in with Mercedes, but he was still thinking about Mitch, Vixen, and the two men, Bellamy and Henderson, that she'd seen with him in Nassau. Since he had Jackie take care of Winston Townson, he wondered if Modesto Colbert sent them to finish the job. He couldn't be sure. Then he took out his phone.

"What's up, Carter?" Geno asked when he answered.

"Where you at?"

"I'm at Romans. What's up?"

"Wait for me. I'll be through there," Carter said and ended the call.

When he arrived at Romans, Geno was in the office waiting for him. He was seated behind Carter's desk and got up when Carter entered the room.

"What's up, Carter?" Geno asked when he walked into the office.

"How's it going, Geno?" Carter replied, sitting down at his desk.

"I'm hanging in there. What's up?" he asked again, and Carter told him about what had taken place at Club Envy.

"My first question is, why'd Vanessa call Angel and Bowie to handle it instead of me?"

"You know I didn't ask. But I think it's because they put in that work for her when the serial killer was on the loose." Carter paused. "But you're right. Her first call should have been to you."

"Not that I got anything against Angel and Bowie; they do good work, but there is a chain of command, you know."

"I know." Carter looked at the pained expression on Geno's face. It was evident that he felt disrespected. "I'll talk to her about it."

"I expected no less."

"But what I wanna know is, did Colbert send these guys to hunt her down and kill her?" Carter asked.

"I'll follow up with Nitty, but I don't think so," Geno told his captain.

"Why not?"

"I think they just recognized her from Nassau and were tying up loose ends. Word on the street is nobody knows why Townson was killed. But like I said, I'll check with Nitty and talk to my sources."

"Let me know what you find out," Carter said and got up.

"Where you on your way to?"

"La Chat."

Geno reached into his pocket and counted out a thousand dollars. "Give that to Mercedes." He handed the money to Carter. "She'll know what it's for."

"So now, I'm your errand boy, huh?"

"Yeah, Carter," Geno said, shaking his head. "Best errand boy in the business."

Carter laughed, gave Geno the finger, and stood up. "And don't you forget it. I'm gone."

Since Mercedes never needed anything, Carter's visit to La Chat was brief. He had a drink, chatted with Mercedes about nothing in particular, and listened to Veronica Rose sing Nina Simone's classic, "My Baby Just Cares for Me," and then he was outta there.

Carter was at Knuckles's spot waiting when Gianna Matisse returned. He was sitting at a table with Knuckles and Kelsey when she entered the establishment. That night, she wore a draped stole minidress by Oscar de la Renta, paired with leather sandals and a matching clutch.

Carter took a sip of his liquor, watching attentively as she went to the cage to get chips for the night. She then walked to the poker table and sat down.

"One thing I'll say for your girl, she be ragging her ass off," Kelsey commented.

"She does," Carter said as he continued to admire her. He looked at Kelsey. "And how did she get to be my girl?"

"That *is* why you're here, right? I mean, you've been here waiting for her to come in for the last hour," Kelsey said. "Am I right?"

Knuckles covered his mouth and looked away. Carter said nothing, but he knew she was right. He just didn't know that he was that obvious.

"Evening, gents." Gianna sat down at the poker table. She looked around and saw that Carter was watching her. She nodded to acknowledge him. "How much is the big blind?" she asked.

"Buy-in twenty grand," Leyla Cardenas said. She had been dealing poker for The Family for more than ten years. "Big blind is fifteen, and the small blind is ten."

Since he was busted, Carter ordered another drink and watched her win. As she played, she occasionally glanced over to see Carter watching her. The one time that their eyes met, Gianna smiled and nodded. Carter raised his glass.

Gianna looked at him as he talked to Knuckles and Kelsey. She could tell that he was watching her. At first, it bothered her.

But he is so fuckin' handsome, Gianna thought. She wondered if he would try to talk to her.

She could tell by the way everybody seemed to bow down to him that he was somebody important, and she wondered if that was going to be good for her or bad for her.

She was coming to Knuckles's joint every night for a reason. And it wasn't to get involved with anybody. Gianna watched him as he talked and laughed with Knuckles and Kelsey.

But he is so goddamn fine, and it has been more than a minute, she thought.

"Ms. Matisse," Leyla said to break her out of the trance that Carter's gaze had her in.

"Huh?"

"It's on you."

"Right," she said and glanced at her cards.

The name of the game was Texas Hold'em. The community cards were the ace of hearts, the king of clubs, jack of spades, four of hearts, and the ten of diamonds.

She tossed in her hand.

"Fold," she said instead of seeing if she could work the flush. With Carter watching intently, Gianna gathered her chips. "That's it for me for the night," she said and stood up. "Could you get somebody to escort me to the cage so I can cash in my chips?"

"Where the fuck do you think you're going with my money?" Sanford, one of the other players, shouted.

"See, there's where you'd be wrong." Gianna smiled. "This is *my* money now. You lost it, so now it's mine. That's how it works."

"Fuck that!" he shouted and bounced out of his chair and pointed at her. "You need to sit your ass down and give me a chance to win back my fuckin' money," he ordered and rushed toward her. When he grabbed her arm, Carter bounced out of his chair and ran toward Gianna to intervene.

"I'd let the lady go if I were you, Sanford."

"Fuck that, Carter. Bitch needs to sit the fuck down and—"

Before he could get another word out, Carter punched him in the face. The punch connected to his jaw, and he dropped like a rock and hit the floor hard.

"Get him outta here," Carter said to Knuckles's men. They picked up Sanford from the floor. "I never wanna see him in here again."

"Yes, Mr. Garrison."

Carter turned to Gianna. "My hero," she said, and his hands shook a bit at the sultry sound of her voice.

"Are you all right?"

"I am now, thank you."

"I would be more than happy to escort you to cash in your chips."

"Thank you."

She handed him the tray, and like any seductress worth her salt, Gianna looped her arm in his.

"Gianna Matisse."

"Carter Garrison."

"It's my pleasure to meet you, Mr. Garrison."

"There's where you'd be wrong, Ms. Matisse," he said, and it caught her off guard. "The pleasure is all mine," he said as they arrived at the cage.

"I stand corrected," she said while they counted her money.

"Can I escort you to your car?"

"Thank you, Mr. Garrison."

"Carter."

"Then you must call me Gianna," she said, putting her money in her clutch before, once again, looping her arm in his. He walked her to her seven-series BMW and held the door open for her to enter.

She rolled down her window. "Thank you."

"Like I said, the pleasure was all mine." Carter paused. "Have dinner with me tomorrow."

"The pleasure would be all mine," Gianna said, and she let out a girlish giggle and wondered where it came from. They exchanged information. "See you tomorrow," she said and drove away, wondering if she was doing the right thing.

Chapter Twenty

It was after two in the morning when Black and Shy arrived in Freeport, and Oscar docked the ship in the Lucayan Harbor. They were fortunate to find a cab that took them to their house at that hour of the morning.

It had been a long day for Shy, starting with a meeting that morning, followed by a rush to pack. She couldn't wait to get in the shower and go to sleep. But first things first.

"I thought you were tired," Black said.

"I'm never *that* tired," Shy replied and crawled into bed with her husband.

When she woke up a few hours later, it was way too early for her. Shy wanted to sleep late like she used to, but those were the days before she took over running her business. Those days, she could sleep until noon and show up at the office when she felt like it.

Now, Shy was out of bed most mornings at seven so she could be in the office at eight thirty. However, lately, she'd been thinking that things were more stable at the office, which meant that Pooja was finally earning her trust. Perhaps she could step back and assume her more traditional position.

She went to the bathroom and was about to get back in bed when the smell of bacon filled her nose. Shy followed the aroma to the kitchen.

"Good morning, Chef."

The startled chef turned around quickly. "Good morning, Mrs. Black."

She walked up to him and hugged Chef. "How have you been?"

"I've been doing all right."

"What about Kya and the kids?"

"She's fine. And the kids eat too much, and why do they keep growing?" Chef laughed.

Shy laughed too. "When you figure that out, let me know."

"Will do."

She looked at all the food that Chef had cooked for them. "I see you went all out as usual."

Chef looked modestly at the food he had cooked for them. "You know how much I love cooking for you, Mrs. Black."

She sat down at the counter in front of the food. "So, what do you have for me?"

"I have pancakes and French toast for you. A ham, spinach, and mushroom quiche, and I have a hash brown casserole." He pointed. "There's Canadian and center-cut bacon, Italian sausage, and steak strips that I marinated overnight and slow-cooked." He kissed his fingers. "They are so tender that they melt in your mouth."

"Everything looks and smells delicious."

"Are you ready to eat?"

"You know I'm always ready to eat."

"Will Mr. Black be joining you?"

Shy paused to think about it. "I should wait for him, shouldn't I?" she said, remembering that this was the romantic getaway she wanted, and then stood up.

"I would. But that's just me. I'm a hopeless romantic."

"Tell you what." Shy smiled and sat down at the table. "Go ahead and make me a little sample plate, and then I'll go see if Michael is up."

After Shy finished eating her sample plate, she said, "Everything was delicious." Then she returned to their bedroom and was surprised that Black wasn't in bed. She could hear the shower, so she went into the bathroom.

"Good morning," she said, immediately finding herself getting caught up by the beads of water against his skin.

"Good morning, Mrs. Black," he said, and watched as Shy disrobed.

Black turned on the second jet in the shower as Shy opened the door and came in. She allowed the water to beat down on her, and then she wet her hair.

"You know I love it when you do that."

"Do what?"

"Wet your hair."

Shy looked at this growing erection. "I see that."

He stepped to her quickly, picked her up, and entered her in one hard, deep thrust. They made slow love against the shower wall until her body shook.

"Ah . . ."

Once they had showered and come out of the bathroom, she asked, "What do you wanna do this morning?"

"I was going to swim a few laps and then eat breakfast."

"I have a counterproposal."

Black sat down on the edge of the bed. "You have my undivided attention, sexy woman."

"I think we should go eat mostly because the food is ready. And then we come back in here, you make me shake, scream, and put me back to sleep. Then you can swim as many laps as you want."

"What makes you think that after you make *me* shake and scream, I won't fall asleep right along with you?"

"I don't," Shy said confidently. "I know I got the skills to put you to sleep, but I didn't want to appear overconfident."

"Whatever," he said, and once they dressed, they went to the kitchen to eat the feast that the chef had prepared for them.

The rest of the morning went the way Shy planned, and when Black woke up later that afternoon, he glanced over at Shy. She was still fast asleep, so he quietly got out of bed and got ready to hit the pool. Their pool was enclosed in an air-conditioned space, and the water temperature was controlled. He dove in.

Once he finished swimming laps, Black got out of the pool and dried himself. He sat by the pool, relaxing, to enjoy the view of the Atlantic Ocean. This was precisely what he had in mind, and he patted himself on the back. Then he picked up the phone and called Chef.

"What can I get for you, Boss?"

"I was in the mood for a pastrami and Swiss sandwich."

"What kind of bread do you want that on?"

"Something like a Kaiser roll."

"I can do that for you," Chef said.

"Great. Do you have any fresh strawberries and blueberries?"

"I do."

"Make me a shake to go with that sandwich, please."

"Will Mrs. Black be joining you?"

"She's still asleep."

"I see. I'll bring that out for you as soon as it's ready."

"Thank you, Chef."

Black had almost finished with his sandwich when Shy joined him at the pool.

"What are you eating?"

"Pastrami and Swiss sandwich on a Kaiser roll. I think Chef just baked the bread. You want one?" he asked and reached for the phone.

"I wouldn't mind having a sandwich, but I was thinking about a Reuben."

Black made the call.

"Yes, Boss?" Chef answered.

"Mrs. Black would like a Reuben."

"Ask her if she wants that made with corned beef or pastrami?"

"Corned beef or pastrami?"

"Both."

"Both," he informed. "What are you drinking?"

"What did you have with yours?"

"Strawberry and blueberry shake. You want one?"

"No, but I know Chef made me some of his famous Bahama Mamas."

"She wants to know if you made her any Bahama Mamas?"

"Of course, I did. Made with fruit that's been soaking since she was last on the island."

"Thanks, Chef." Black ended the call and glanced at Shy. "He got you."

Once Shy had finished eating, they went down to the beach and took a long walk, holding hands as they walked along the edge of the water.

That night, Chef prepared grilled porterhouse steak with lobster tails and truffle butter, along with potatoes au gratin, stir-fried spinach with garlic, and a crisp and creamy Caesar salad.

Shy wanted to make it romantic, so they dressed for dinner. She dug around her closet and wore a Bottega Veneta V-neck gown that she'd had for years. Knowing his wife the way he did, Black planned for this and packed an Armani silk tuxedo.

They dined by candlelight in their dining room and sipped champagne with their meal. After dinner, Mr. and Mrs. Black retired to their room and had drinks on their balcony. Things were moving along in a way that made Black think they were going to retire to bed for another night of lovemaking.

However, once again, Shy had other ideas.

"You know what I wanna do tonight?" she asked.

"I don't, but I know you're going to tell me."

Shy kissed him on the cheek. "I wanna go dancing."

"Of course, you do."

So, after they changed into something more comfortable, they went dancing at the Barcode Lounge and the Bones Bar.

When they returned home, they retired to their room. Shy opened the French doors to allow the warm Caribbean breeze to fill the room. Admiring the softness of his wife's skin, Black slid his hand across her chest. He took one of her nipples into his mouth. She held his head while he squeezed her other breast. She kissed him gently. His kiss was long and tender. Her breath got caught in her throat as he kissed her.

"I love you, baby," he whispered.

"I love you too."

He kissed her again, this time with more passion. His hand pushed between her thighs and touched her. She was ready; she was always ready for him. His tongue slid inside of her and sucked her moist lips gently. Her body began to quiver as he licked her clit with the tip of his tongue. Her head drifted back; her thighs pressed together as her body convulsed from the circles he made.

He looked at her. She was still the most beautiful woman that he had ever known. He loved her with every fiber of his being, and he wanted to be inside her all the time. He guided himself in her, and her body enveloped him in warmth and soft wetness.

"Ah," he breathed out.

She looked into his eyes and could feel the love that he had for her. Her mouth opened wide as he thrust in and out of her slowly, but it was hard and deep, just the way she loved it. She wrapped her legs around his waist and tossed her body into his. Her toes curled, and Shy screamed and rippled around his pounding length. He sucked her earlobe, and she shattered.

She couldn't handle it any longer. She kneeled and ran her hands over his body, stroking him and enjoying the feeling of his hard dick in her hand. Next, she smiled and began running her tongue around the head and along the sides of his shaft before she took him into her mouth.

Next, she got up on the bed and eased herself down on it. She moaned with pleasure while continuing to slide up and down on his shaft. She got so caught up that she screamed his name while slamming her body against his. She rode him harder, working her hips and inner muscles until he began to swell and explode inside of her. Finally, she screamed and collapsed on his chest.

"I love you, baby," he said in a whisper.

"I love you too."

Chapter Twenty-one

It was a different type of day for Carter Garrison. He had a date that night with Gianna Matisse. It had been a long time since he stepped out with a woman. He did a lot of fuckin', but dating, not so much. She was the most beautiful woman he had ever seen, surpassing even Millena. He agonized over what to wear. He knew that Gianna had changed her name, so he decided not to ask her any questions. However, the fact that she'd done so intrigued him, adding to the allure. Carter wanted her, so he thought about how aggressive he should be.

They arranged to have a late dinner at Nourriture Fanatique, an old-fashioned French bistro on the Lower East Side with exposed brick and oversized windows. A long room with globe lights and marble tables provided ambiance. The menu featured a mix of typical bistro classics and newly inspired dishes.

Carter arrived at Nourriture Fanatique just before ten o'clock. He sat at the bar, ordered a drink, and waited impatiently for her arrival. He looked at his watch; it was ten o'clock. By a quarter to eleven, Carter had finished his third drink and called for the check. He paid the tab, left a twenty tip, and rose to leave. That's when Gianna arrived.

"Good evening, Carter. Have you been waiting long?" she said as if she were only a minute or two late.

"About an hour."

Carter wasn't sure which emotion was stronger, the anger he felt about waiting so long for her to show up, or the joy that she was standing in front of him. So, he settled on the combination.

"I hate waiting, but you were worth the wait." Carter looked her over from head to toe. "You look incredible tonight," he said of the expensive, abstract orchid satin cocktail dress and satin sandals she wore.

"Thank you very much, Carter. You're looking very handsome yourself," she complimented him. "How long have you been waiting?" Gianna asked.

"About an hour."

"Sorry to keep you waiting," she said, looking at her diamond watch. "I had a prior engagement that took longer than I expected." Gianna smiled, making his dick perk up a little. "I am sorry, Carter. But I tell you what." She reached out and touched his hand. "I promise to be a fascinating dinner conversationalist. But I think it's only fair to warn you that I'm a sucker for an intelligent conversation."

"So am I," he replied.

They were escorted to a table, and shortly after that, the waiter arrived to take drink orders.

"Hennessy Paradis, straight up." Carter looked at Gianna. Her eyes were driving him insane.

"And the lady will have?"

"I'll have a Paloma."

"Excellent choice."

The waiter brought out the drinks and took their order for dinner. The poulet rôti, which was roast chicken served with pommes purée for Gianna, while Carter ordered the onglet au poivre, which was hanger steak. The two talked their way through dinner, actually doing more talking than eating.

When the wait staff broke out the vacuum cleaner, they took the hint that it was time to leave.

"What's wrong?" Carter asked.

Gianna took a deep breath. "I'm not ready to go yet. And I don't want the evening to end," she replied.

"Then why are you?"

Gianna smiled. "What did you have in mind?"

Soon, they were checking into a suite at the Sixty LES, a hotel on Allen Street. Carter crawled on his hands and knees above Gianna and kissed all over her body. He paused to lick and suck her pert nipples. Her clit was throbbing by the time he moved on to suck her neck. Then he took her nipple into his mouth and shoved her legs apart again. He slid his body between her thighs, and she felt his lips against her clit. He hungrily sucked her clit, while squeezing her nipple. She was rocking her hips back and forth.

"Yes, yes!" she screamed, and her head drifted back as he plunged deeper inside her. She felt another orgasm building. "I'm coming . . ."

She knelt, placing her ass in the air in front of him. He pulled her hips up and thrust himself inside her. She lay there, squeezing her nipples until her body started to tremble.

"Fuck me, fuck me," she chanted.

Carter squeezed her cheeks and slammed his body into hers, and then he brought her to a gut-wrenching orgasm. Then he pulled out of her, grabbed her shoulders, and entered her again in one hard thrust. After he let released her shoulders, he squeezed her tit with one hand, while reaching between her legs. Finally, he slowed his pace and began to long stroke her, pulling almost completely out of her and then slowly easing himself back inside of her.

Instantly, his entire body went rigid. He thought about the last time he had sex without a condom and pulled out of her. She jerked his load before collapsing on the bed.

Chapter Twenty-two

After dancing the night away with Shy, Black woke up the following morning feeling relaxed and refreshed. Of course, Shy was still asleep, so he quietly got out of bed and got ready to hit the pool. On his way out, he stopped in the kitchen to greet Chef. He had already cooked breakfast and was relaxing while he thought about dinner preparations.

"Morning, Chef."

"Morning, Mike. You ready to eat?"

"No. Cassandra is still sleeping."

Chef laughed. "I was surprised to see her up so early yesterday."

"She got a business to run, so she gets up earlier these days. But we went out last night, so it might be afternoon before she surfaces."

"*That's* the Mrs. Black I know."

"Yeah, me too. But I'm getting used to the new one."

"Well, if it's gonna be afternoon, I might make some other things I know she likes and call it brunch."

"I'm sure she'll love that. I'm gonna hit the pool. See you later."

After he finished swimming, Black went inside to find Shy awake but still in bed. As he thought it would be, it was after noon.

"Hi, baby."

"Did you have a good swim?"

"I did. You just waking up?"

"Long enough to notice you were gone and use the bathroom. Then I got back into bed."

"I'm surprised you aren't in the kitchen."

"It wasn't easy. I think it was the smell of food that woke me up. But I wanted to wait and eat with you."

"I'm gonna jump in the shower, wash some of this chlorine off of me, and then we can go eat." They both showered and made love, then dressed and went to the kitchen.

In addition to the usual array of breakfast foods, Chef had prepared pot roast hash, eggs Benedict casserole, orange pecan French toast, sausage enchiladas, cinnamon rolls, and pineapple sunrise mimosas.

"Hi, Chef."

"Good afternoon, Mrs. Black."

"Everything looks and smells delicious," she said, taking a plate.

"I hope you enjoy it."

"I'm sure I will."

After they stuffed themselves on the delicious meal Chef had prepared, a question arose.

"What did wanna do now?" Black asked his lovely wife.

She giggled. "I wanna go back to sleep. But if all I do down here is eat and sleep, I'll be as big as a house."

"Nonsense. You eat like a horse, and look at you. Still fine as hell."

"Thank you, Michael, but let's go for a walk on the beach instead."

"I'm with you," he said, and they were off to the beach.

They walked hand in hand along the water's edge, talking a little of this, a little of that, and enjoying just being together. Shy looked at the man walking alongside her and could honestly say that she was more in love with him now than she was all those years ago.

"Do you remember the first time we walked on the beach?" she asked.

"How could I forget? It was this beach, and you tried to prove how slow you were and that you couldn't catch a cold." He laughed. "And then you seduced me."

"You know you wanted it."

"I did. Still do."

They walked the beach in silence. "This was such a good idea. I really needed this," Shy said and squeezed his hand a little tighter.

"You know I live to make you happy. I'd do anything for you."

"I think you've proven that time and time again. And I love you so much. You make me feel so special."

"That's because you *are* special. Very special to me."

When they returned to their house, Chef had made them another pitcher of pineapple sunrise mimosas, and they decided to sit by the pool and enjoy each other's company when the doorbell suddenly rang. A surprised Mr. and Mrs. Black looked at each other.

"Who could that be?" she asked.

"I don't know. Nobody is supposed to know we're here," Black said.

Shy got up and went to check the front door monitor.

"It's Napoleon. What's he doing here?"

"I don't know. Nobody is supposed to know we're here," Black repeated.

Shy was going to get the pitcher of mimosas Chef had made for them when the doorbell rang again.

"I'll get it."

"No. If we don't answer, maybe he'll just go away," Black chuckled.

"That wouldn't be right. And besides, it's Napoleon."

"Right. He won't give up and go away," Black said as the doorbell rang a third time. "Eventually, he'll hop the fence and come back here to look in the windows."

When Shy returned to the pool with a pitcher of mimosas, Napoleon was with her.

"Afternoon, Boss."

"What's up, Napoleon? How you been?"

"I'm excellent."

"What are you doing here?"

"I needed to talk to you."

"How did you know we were here?"

"You took your wife dancing last night."

Black chuckled. "I thought I was being low profile. Incognito."

Napoleon and Shy laughed.

"How many times me hear you tell Rain that a hat and dark sunglasses are *not* a disguise?" Napoleon inquired.

"Told you," Shy said, giggling.

Black smiled, but he said nothing.

"You know who you look like in a hat and dark sunglasses, Boss?"

"Who?" Black asked.

"Mike Black in a hat and dark sunglasses," Napoleon said, and Shy laughed.

"So, why are you here?"

"Donald Pinkney is dead."

"How?"

"Somebody shot him," Napoleon said. "They found him body at a house in Fortune Cay."

"Take me to the body."

"So much for the 'little vacation,'" Shy said because somehow, she knew that this was going to happen.

Napoleon drove Black and Shy out on Midshipman Highway to Conard Street. As they drove up, Black could see that several of his men were standing or sitting outside the house. The ones who were sitting down stood up when Napoleon got out of the car. All of the men literally stood at attention when Black got out and held the door open for Shy. They went into the house, speaking to the men as they passed.

"Where's the body?" Black asked.

One of his men pointed toward the rear of the house. "Back here," he said and led the way. "I was supposed to meet him here. This what I find when I arrived."

He opened the door, and they stepped into the bedroom. There was blood everywhere, on the floor and the walls. The room was ransacked like it had been searched, and there were signs of a struggle. In the middle of it all was the body of Donald Pinkney. His clothes were bloody, and an ax was still in his head.

"My God," Shy said and turned away.

Black turned to his men. "Any idea who did this?"

"No, sir."

"Find out," Black said, and then he escorted Shy out of the house.

"You want me to take you back to the house?" Napoleon asked.

"No. Take me to Mr. Elgin," Black said as he held the car door open for Shy.

Napoleon drove the Blacks to the Port Lucaya Marina. Since he had a stroke years earlier, each morning, Mr. Elgin walked from his home to Port Lucaya Marina, where he spent the day talking shit with the fishing boat operators.

When the boss of The Family walked into the place, all conversation stopped, and the men happily greeted their leader. Mr. Elgin was seated in the back of the room, where he waited patiently for Black and Shy to get to him.

"Good morning, Mr. Elgin," Shy said.

He rose to his feet, bowed at the waist, and kissed Shy's hand.

"As always, Mrs. Black, it is my pleasure to see you."

He turned to Black and shook his hand. "Knuckle nibbler," Black joked. "How are you, old man?"

"Not bad for an old man."

"You look great, Mr. Elgin," Shy said.

"Why, thank you, Mrs. Black. That is quite the compliment coming from the most beautiful woman on the planet." He kissed her hand again.

"You trying to mack my wife, old man?" Black asked.

"Of course not. I'm as helpless as a kitten in a tree."

"Kittens in trees still have claws," Black said.

"This is true, but not in this case." Mr. Elgin paused. "You hear about Pink?"

"What can you tell me about that?" Black asked.

"Pink was having money problems after his wife, Caroline, got tired of his meandering ways, and she left him."

"'Bout time," Napoleon quipped.

"That morning, she handed him a paper and tell him he must sign." He laughed. "Of course, Caroline, she don't tell him he is signing their divorce papers."

"Of course not," Napoleon commented. "Why would she tell him that?"

"Once him sign it, Caroline, she send him off to work, and after him gone, Caroline, she pack up she things and head straight to the bank to drain them accounts of all of them money." Mr. Elgin laughed. "She next stop was the airport. I heard she's somewhere in Miami."

"That's a shame," Black said because he wanted to talk to her.

Mr. Elgin held up one finger. "Here is the thing. After this, Donald him desperate for money, but it doesn't take long before him have a new woman, and him have plenty of cash."

"Any idea where this cash is coming from?"

"Cocaine. Him and him cousin, Barick."

"Where can we find him?" Shy asked.

"McLean's Town Cay."

Shy looked at Black. "Isn't that where you were when you got shot?"

Black patted her hand. "Yes, it was." He stood up and extended his hand. "Thank you, Mr. Elgin."

"Anytime, Mike."

"Good to see you, Mr. Elgin," Shy said and kissed him on the cheek.

"The pleasure was, of course, all mine, Mrs. Black," Mr. Elgin said.

Black, Shy, and Napoleon got into the car and made the hour's drive to McLean's Town Cay. After stopping at the Tipsy Sisters, they were told where Barick lived. They drove out there, got out of the car, and approached the house. As they got closer, Barick fired a shot at Black's feet.

"That's far enough!" Barick shouted.

Black, Shy, and Napoleon stopped and put up their hands.

"State your business!" Barick shouted.

"I'm Mike Black."

Barick fired again.

"I know who you are! State your business!"

"I wanted to ask you about your cousin, Donald."

"He's dead, and we have no business. Now, get off my property!"

As they began to back away, someone fired a shot that came close to hitting Shy. Black pulled both of his guns and began firing as they retreated to better cover behind their car.

"Get behind me!" he shouted to Shy.

Shy quickly got behind him, and Black continued firing until they reached cover.

"You okay?"

"I'm all right," Shy said, reaching into her purse and taking out the PLR22.

"You okay, Napoleon?"

"I'm good."

"How many clips do you have, Cassandra?"

"Three."

"Cover us."

Shy stood up and began firing at the house as Black and Napoleon came out from cover and ran toward the building. When they made it, Shy reloaded.

"Ready?"

"Ready, Boss," Napoleon said, and he kicked in the door.

Black rushed into the house, and Napoleon came in behind him. Black saw Barick and another man standing there. Barick had a rifle, and the other man was armed with a 357 Magnum. When Barick raised the weapon, Black fired and hit him with a shot to the chest. The other man fired at Napoleon as he ran toward the back door. His shot missed, and Napoleon returned fire, hitting him with two shots in the back as he tried to get away.

"You all right?" Black asked.

"I'm okay, Boss."

"That didn't go the way I wanted it to," Black said as they walked out of the house.

"Perhaps. But Barick was a stupid man, so it went exactly the way I thought it would," Napoleon said as they reached their car.

Chapter Twenty-three

When they returned to Freeport, they went to see Donald's new woman, Lena. She cleaned rooms at the Lighthouse Pointe at Grand Lucayan Resort. While Black and Napoleon sat outside by the pool, Shy went inside to ask for Lena. When Shy found her, she told Lena that Mike Black was at the pool and wanted to speak with her.

Lena looked at Shy. Although she had never seen, much less met, Black's wife, she heard the stories of the gun-stinging, ex-drug dealer who couldn't be killed.

"What's this about?"

"He wants to talk to you about your friend Donald Pinkney."

"I need to finish cleaning this room, and then I'll take my break."

"I'll be right here," Shy said and sat down. "It's not that I don't trust you . . . Let me stop lying. I *don't* trust you, so I'll be right here until you get done."

Now, she *was* scared.

Lena went back to work, but Shy noticed that her hands were shaking.

"You don't have to be afraid. I'm not gonna hurt you. I promise, we just wanna talk."

"Okay," Lena said, but it didn't change anything. She was still frightened.

When Lena finished the room, she told her supervisor that she was going on break and went to the pool with Shy. Both Black and Napoleon stood up when they saw the ladies coming.

"Lena?" Black asked.

She nodded.

"Please have a seat." Black waited until everyone sat down before he did.

"I know that you're working, so I won't take up much of your time."

"Okay."

"First of all, I need to tell you that we found Donald this morning. He was murdered last night."

"Oh my God," Lena said in shock and began to cry.

"I'm very sorry for your loss," Shy said, and Napoleon nodded respectfully.

As Lena's tears flowed at the loss of her man, Shy rubbed her back, trying to comfort her. She looked at Black and bravely wiped away her tears.

"Do you know who did it?" Lena asked.

"No. I'm sorry, but I don't. I was hoping that you could tell me that."

"No, I don't know who murdered him." Lena paused, and her tears flowed a little harder. "I knew the kind of man Pink was when I met him and the kind of business he was in, so I knew this could happen." She got quiet. "That one day, somebody would come to tell me he was dead. I thought I was prepared for it. But I'm not." Her tears flowed again. "I'm not even close to being prepared."

"Anything that you can tell me would be helpful," Black said.

"I know that Pink was involved with Barick and a man named Lewis Huber."

"We are aware of Barick," Napoleon said. "But not the other man."

"What can you tell me about him?" Black asked.

"Not much. I know that he works for Jada West in Nassau," Lena said, and Shy got that feeling in her stomach that she felt anytime Jada's name was mentioned.

"I don't know what they were doing, but I can tell you that him and Lewis were involved with somebody from New York that I never met, but they talked about him all the time."

"Was his name Mitch?" Black questioned.

"I think that's him," Lena said, but she couldn't be sure.

"Thank you, Lena," Black said and stood up. "Again, I am very sorry for your loss."

"If there's anything you need," Shy began, and she stood up. "Please call me."

"Thank you, Mrs. Black."

After that, Napoleon drove Black and Shy back to their house. Once they were packed, they called Jake and told him they were going to Nassau. They were aboard the jet, and Jake was going through preflight checks for their flight to Nassau when Napoleon got on the plane.

"Where are you going?" Black asked.

"With you." Napoleon raised one finger. "And before you say anything else, Boss, I have already spoken with the boss of The Family. Ms. Robinson said that she was very disappointed to hear that you were down here without her knowledge and without a bodyguard."

Black and Shy glanced at each other and smiled.

"She insisted that I drop whatever I was doing and not let you two out of my sight."

"Glad to have you, Napoleon," Shy said.

"I'll call Rain when we get to Nassau," Black said.

"It will be like old times," Napoleon commented and took a seat.

Upon arrival in Nassau, they went to Lewis Huber's apartment. As they approached, Black saw that the door was ajar. Once they had their guns out, Black kicked open the door, and they went in slowly.

"Split up," Black said. "And stay alert."

"I'll check outside," Napoleon said and went out the back door.

After looking around the front room, Shy went to check the bedrooms.

"Back here, Michael."

When Black entered the room, Shy pointed. She found Lewis dead. He was hog-tied and shot in the back of the head.

"That's not good," Black said.

"No, it's not," Shy stated and walked out of the room. "He won't be answering any questions today."

"Not tomorrow either."

"What now?"

"Search the place," Black said as Napoleon entered the house.

"I didn't see anything outside. What about you fellows?"

"We found Lewis. He's dead," Shy said as she searched. "He's in the bedroom."

Napoleon went to check the body before he joined the search. While they searched the apartment, Shy found a note about a meeting.

"Where and when?" Black asked.

"The meeting was at Lynden Pindling Airport in hangar 18," Shy said, and the three left the apartment and headed back to the airport.

When they arrived at the hangar, they approached and saw that there were three men inside, but they couldn't hear what they were saying.

"I need to get in there so I can hear them," Black said and started for the door. Shy was right behind him.

"Where are you going?"

"With you."

"Right." He looked at Shy. "I guess I can't convince you to wait here, can I?"

"No."

Black shook his head and went inside, where they hid behind a row of fifty-gallon drums.

"We've taken care of Mitch, Pinkney, and Lewis," they heard one say.

"Only one more loose end to tie up," another man said.

"What are you standing around here for? Get to it."

"As soon as she's gassed up, I'll be on my way," the man replied and walked toward the plane.

Black looked at Shy. "I think we need to be on that plane, Michael."

"I think you're right," Black said and wanted to tell her to stay with Napoleon, but he knew his wife.

"Napoleon is gonna be mad," Shy said as they approached the plane and got on it to stow away.

Napoleon's eyes opened wide as he watched them sneak onto the plane. He panicked as the plane taxied out of the hangar and prepared for takeoff.

As he watched the plane taxi down the runway, Napoleon got out his phone and called Jake.

"What's up?"

"The boss and Mrs. Black have stowed away aboard a jet, and I have no idea where they are going."

Jake laughed. "You mean you lost them again?"

When he was Shy's bodyguard, she turned losing Napoleon into an art form.

"Not funny, Jake."

"Don't worry, Napoleon."

"What do you mean, 'Don't worry'? Didn't you hear what I said? The boss them on a plane heading for God only knows where, and you say, 'Don't worry'?"

"Right. Mr. and Mrs. Black can take care of themselves. Whenever they land, I'm sure they'll let you know where they are."

"Okay," Napoleon said and tried his best to calm down.

"There is one thing you can do while you wait for them to call you."

"What's that?"

"Call Monika. She told me once that she can find them anywhere in the world."

"Good idea. That's a great idea," Napoleon said excitedly. "First useful thing you've said all day. I'll call you when I know something," Napoleon said and put in a call to Monika. She was out of the country, but Carla was there.

She laughed.

"Lost them again, huh?"

"This is *not* funny, Carla," Napoleon shouted.

"Don't worry, Napoleon. I can track them."

"Thank you, Carla."

"No worries, Napoleon. Their current location is 23°14'03.3 "N 64°34'25.9"W."

Napoleon chuckled. "I don't mean to sound unappreciative, but where is that, Carla?"

"They are somewhere over the North Atlantic Ocean heading south. I will let you know when and where they land."

"Carla, you're the greatest."

"I know."

Chapter Twenty-four

When Black and Shy landed, they had no idea where they were. They stayed in hiding on the plane until they no longer heard men talking. Once they got off the plane and left the hangar, they found out that they were in Barbados at Grantley Adams International Airport. Since it was too late to follow the men, and they had no idea where they were going, they caught a cab to the Wyndham Grand Barbados Sam Lords Castle, an All-Inclusive Resort.

Black's first call was to Napoleon.

"Where are you?" Black asked when he answered.

"It's me who should be asking you where *you* are," Napoleon replied.

"We're in Barbados at the Wyndham Grand Barbados Sam Lords Castle Resort. Where are you?"

"With Jake aboard the Cessna."

"Good. Tell Jake to take off and come for us."

"What did you find in Barbados?"

"Nothing yet. We just got here."

His next call was to Jada.

"Rumor has it that you and Mrs. Black are on the island."

"We were, but now we're in Barbados."

"What, pray tell, are you doing in Barbados?"

"Following up on something."

"Am I permitted to know what you are following up on?"

"Are you familiar with a man named Lewis Huber?"

"I am. He works at the dock with Oscar."

"We found him dead in his apartment earlier this afternoon."

"I see."

"How much of an organization do you have here in Barbados?"

"Not much. I have two ladies and a gentleman who facilitates their activities as needed. Not much of a market there."

"I see."

"Am I permitted to know any other details that you can speak of?"

"The word I got is that Lewis Huber and Donald Pinkney, who works for Napoleon in Freeport, were into something along with Mitchell Wright and, I'm guessing, somebody on this island."

"I see. I doubt it's one of the ladies, but you never know. I'll reach out to them and Conrad Boyle. He's the man who I told you facilitates their activities."

"We're at the Wyndham. I'll wait to hear from you."

"Splendid," Jada said and ended the call.

"What did she say?"

"That she doesn't have much of an operation here. What she has here is connections and two women, but no real organization. She's gonna reach out to them and get back to me."

With time on their hands, Black and Shy resigned themselves to relax, enjoy the island, and see what happens next. Black called Napoleon to let him know what was going on.

"How much of an operation does Ms. West have there?" Napoleon inquired.

"Ms. West has two ladies who live on the island and who work the hotels and resorts, as well as Conrad Boyle."

"I know him," Napoleon said. "He's an event manager at the O2 Beach Club and Spa."

"You know anything else about him? Like, was he involved with Mitch and them?"

"That, I cannot say with any certainty."

"You and Jake in the air?"

"Not yet. He has submitted a flight plan and is awaiting clearance to take off."

"Okay. Let me know when you land."

"I will do," Napoleon said, and Black ended the call.

"What do you wanna do while we wait for someone to get back to us?" Black asked.

"I want to take a shower. It was so dirty on that plane, and then I wanna eat," Shy said, undressing as she sashayed to the bathroom.

"Need company?"

"Always."

Black followed behind his wife, taking off his clothes as he walked into the bathroom. Since they had no luggage, they had to put on their dirty clothes and left their suite.

The resort had three places to eat. There was the Mediterranean Market, which featured Mediterranean cuisine from Portugal, Spain, Greece, and North Africa. The Castle View served unique Caribbean gourmet dishes with a twist from their steak and seafood bars. And Sam Lord's Grill by the pool.

"Burgers, quesadillas?" Shy frowned and shook her head. "I don't think so," she said after looking at the available places to eat. "Let's check out their steak and seafood bars at Castle View."

"Castle View it is," Black said, and they went to eat.

Mr. and Mrs. Black had just sat down to dine on their food when Shy got a phone call from a private number. Since she didn't accept unknown calls, Shy didn't answer. When the phone began ringing shortly after that, she answered.

"Who is this?"

"Good evening, Shy. Jada West speaking."

"Hello, Jada."

"I apologize for calling on your phone, but Mr. Black isn't answering his."

"He probably left his phone in the room. He does it all the time."

"And it is so annoying."

"Tell me about it."

"How much time do you have?" Jada giggled, and so did Shy. "Anyway, the ladies are fine; however, I was not able to contact Conrad Boyle."

"Conrad Boyle," Shy said, and Black looked up. "He's the man who facilitates the ladies, right?"

"Yes. May I send his address to your phone?"

"Of course, you can."

"Sending it now," Jada paused. "He also works as an event manager at O2 Beach Club and Spa."

"Got it," Shy said when she received Jada's text.

"I also sent you an image of Conrad."

"That would be helpful," Shy said, and seconds later, she received the text. "Got it. We'll check them out."

"Thank you, Shy."

"Anytime, Jada."

"Please let me know if you find him."

"I will call you as soon as we know something," Shy said and ended the call.

"What did she say?" Black asked.

"That it's annoying when you leave your phone," Shy giggled.

"Ha-ha. Jada got jokes. What else did she say about Conrad Boyle and the ladies she has working here?"

"Jada said that the ladies are fine, but she hasn't been able to contact Boyle. She sent his address and a picture of him."

"That's helpful."

"I know. She said that he works at the O2 Beach Club and Spa."

"I know. Napoleon told me." Black picked up his fork. "As soon as we finish eating, we'll go to the resort."

"Honestly—" Shy took a bite of her shrimp. "I don't think we're gonna find him at the resort."

"Neither do I."

"And I think we're gonna find him dead when we get to his house."

"So do I."

After they finished eating, they paid their tab, left their server a healthy tip, and left Castle View.

"Not so fast, young man," Shy said.

"What?"

Shy pointed toward the elevators. "Go get your phone." She sat down in the hotel lobby and crossed her legs. "I'll be right here when you get back."

Once Black returned to the lobby holding up his phone, Shy stood up, and they left the resort. They caught a cab to O2 Beach Club and Spa. When they arrived at the beach club, they were informed that Conrad Doyle was not at work that evening, nor had he been at work for three days. Shy was able to find someone who worked with Boyle, and she also worked as an event manager at the beach club.

"The last night he was here, he got a call that really shook him. He left after that, and that was the last time I saw him."

"Do you know who he was talking to?" Shy asked.

"No, I'm sorry."

"Did he say anything before he left?"

"Yes. When he got off the phone, I knew something was wrong, so I asked him what the matter was. He said he was in deep shit and asked me to cover his event. He rushed out of here after that."

"Did he say where he was going or what it was about?"

"No, he didn't. Is he in some kind of trouble?"

"That's what we're trying to find out. Thank you for your time," Shy said, and they left the O2 Beach Club and Spa. They caught a cab to the address that Shy got from Jada. When they got to his house, every light in the house that was visible from the street was on.

"That is never good," Shy said as she reached into her purse for her Beretta. Once she made sure there was one in the chamber, she and Black slowly approached the house.

Shy rang the bell.

"Mr. Doyle!" she shouted. "I'm a friend of Jada West!"

When she got no response, Shy tried the doorknob. "It's not locked."

Black raised his weapons and went inside, with Shy following behind him.

"You wanna split up?" Shy asked.

"No. Not this time. Let's stay together. I got a bad feeling about this place."

Shy kissed him on the cheek. "And then I go and spoil it all by saying something stupid like I love you."

It was a line from "Somethin' Stupid," an old song by Frank Sinatra. Ever since they took in Sandy Hackett's Rat Pack Show, which featured impersonators of Frank Sinatra, Dean Martin, Sammy Davis Jr., and Joey Bishop while they were in Vegas to kill Jacara Delbridge, who was involved in Shy's kidnapping and captivity, it had become an inside joke between them.

It didn't take long for Black and Shy to find Conrad Boyle's body. He had been hog-tied and shot in the back of the head.

"Just like Lewis Huber," Shy said.

"Nothing else to do but clear the house and get outta here."

They didn't find anything helpful in their search, so after they wiped down everything they had touched, Black and Shy left the house, and since they had no luggage, they took a cab back to the airport to wait for Jake and Napoleon to arrive.

"Where are we going, Boss?" Jake asked when Black and Shy got on the jet.

"Nassau."

Chapter Twenty-five

It was past ten o'clock that evening when Carter arrived at Romans to continue making his rounds. When he woke up in the hotel that morning, Gianna was gone. Since he was in no hurry, he picked up the phone and ordered room service. Once he had placed his order, he got out of bed and headed for the bathroom to take a long, hot shower. While the water beat down on his neck and back, he closed his eyes, and his mind replayed highlights of the night he spent with Gianna.

She began to stroke him slowly, moving her hands up and down. Up and down, deeper and deeper, slowly . . . until she had taken almost all of him in her mouth.

"Shit," Carter said and grabbed a handful of the sheet. She looked deeply into his eyes, taking him to the back of her throat.

He pulled her on top of him, and she straddled him, wiggling her hips and moving her body slowly until she had adjusted herself to his size and taken him all in. Her body began to quiver, and she tried to roll off him.

"Fuck you think you going?" Carter asked, grabbing her ass.

She was moving her body up and down and side to side. He pulled forward and began rubbing her nipples before taking one into his mouth. Next, she started to move her hips faster. He felt his dick expand, and he pushed it into her harder. Then he felt her body begin to shake.

"I'm coming!" she yelled, and her head drifted back, and he felt her drenching him with her juices, and she practically jumped out of bed.

Suddenly, someone knocked at the door, bringing him back to reality.

"Room Service."

"Be right there," Carter shouted and turned off the water.

He wrapped a towel around his waist, draped another across his shoulders, and went to answer the door.

"Oh," the attendant said, and she smiled at Carter. "Room Service."

Carter opened the door wider. "Come on in."

As she wheeled the cart into the room, Carter got his pants and took out some money. He handed her a twenty-dollar bill because it was the smallest bill he had.

"Thank you," she said gladly and left the room, closing the door behind her.

After he finished eating, he got dressed and went home to change. He prided himself on his appearance, so he didn't mind spending money to look his best at all times. Much of the time, when you saw Carter Garrison, he was wearing a suit, which was tailor-made for him. Whether he had a matching tie depended on the outfit and occasion.

He laid out a midnight-blue plaid suit that he planned to wear with a light blue, pin-striped shirt and ties. His shoes were Alessandro Demésure leather oxfords. Once he was dressed, Carter left the condo. He went around to all of the legitimate businesses that he controlled, as well as the illegal companies that operated during the day.

It was his routine, and he very rarely broke it. However, this day was different. Not that he did anything different, but it was his state of mind that was different. Carter couldn't get Gianna Matisse out of his thoughts. Not since Millena Hayes had a woman captivated his attention the way Gianna had in such a short time. He gave some thought to exactly why that was. He had known and been with many women in his life and thought that no one could replace the way he felt about Millena.

Was it her sex? he asked himself.

No, he answered.

Even though they only had sex that one time, he hadn't stopped thinking about it. Not even Rain Robinson, whom he could honestly say was the best sex he'd ever had, could compare to what he was feeling for Gianna.

Or is it the mystery of who she really is that's got you so captivated?

He took some time to think about it.

Yeah, that's it, he surmised.

"Carter!" Geno shouted to bring him out of the trance that Gianna had him in.

"Huh?"

"There's somebody here to see you," Geno said and pointed to a woman that Carter had never seen before.

"Right. Who is she?"

"Her name is Tabitha Potter."

"What does she want?"

"She said that she had a problem she needed help with. I didn't ask what it was."

"Thanks," Carter said and walked over to where the woman was waiting to speak with him. "Ms. Potter?"

"Yes."

"My name is Carter Garrison. I understand you've got a problem that I might be able to help you with."

"Yes, yes, I do." She stood up and shook Carter's hand. "And thank you for seeing me."

"Let's talk in my office," he said and led the way. Geno followed him in. "If it's all right with you, Mr. Crocker is gonna sit in on our conversation today," he said as he sat at his desk. "Is that all right?"

“That’s fine.” Tabitha sat down and nervously fiddled with her hands.

“Can I get you anything?” Geno asked.

“No, thank you, I’m fine,” she replied. She had never done anything like this before, and she was scared. But her anger overruled her fear.

“Why don’t you tell me what I can do for you?”

“I met a man online about nine months ago. He said his name was Harvey Davenport.” She smiled. “We chatted online for a while, and we just clicked. We had so much in common, and I began to feel like he was the perfect man for me. We moved in together after three months, and we got married a month ago. Then he disappeared.”

“Disappeared?”

“Yes. One morning, he went to work, and that was the last time I saw him. I called the police and reported him missing, but I never heard anything back from them.”

“Typical,” Geno spat out. He never had any use for the cops.

“But after a couple of days, I began getting overdraft notices from my bank.” Her smile disappeared, and her anger came roaring out. “Come to find out, that the bastard withdrew all of my money.”

“How much money are we talking about?”

“One hundred seventy-five thousand dollars that I got as a settlement for a wrongful death lawsuit that I filed on behalf of my mother.”

Carter and Geno looked at each other. “I see. Go on,” Carter encouraged.

“I reported it to the police, and they investigated. They got surveillance from the bank, and sure enough, it was Harvey who withdrew the money. But when they went to his job to arrest him, the office was empty.” A single tear rolled down her cheek. “And they couldn’t find any evidence that the business ever existed.”

"I am so sorry that happened to you," Carter said sympathetically.

"I was heartbroken and devastated. I loved him, and I thought he loved me, but it was all a con to get my money. I felt like such a fool." She wiped her single tear. "It's like that old saying, a fool and her money are soon separated," she chuckled, but it was forced. "That's me."

"I really am so sorry about this," Carter repeated.

"I saw him a couple of weeks ago."

"Did you confront him?"

"No. He was with another woman, so I followed him."

"Smart girl," Geno said.

"Can you help me try to get my money back, Mr. Garrison?"

"I can't promise you anything, but I will do what I can to help you."

"Thank you so much, sir."

Carter stood up, and so did Geno. "You're welcome. Just give all the information you have to Mr. Crocker, and he'll see you out."

Once she had given Geno all he requested, he escorted her out of the office.

"What do you think is up with that?" Geno asked when he came back into the office.

"Sounds to me that this wasn't his first time doing this," Carter said. "I'd bet money on it."

"And I'd take some of that action."

"See what you can do for her," Carter said and walked out with Geno. "Put somebody good on it."

"You got it. Where are you on your way to?"

"Shooters," Carter said and left Romans.

After making stops at Shooters, La Chat, and Club Envy, Carter arrived at Knuckles's spot. He looked around for Gianna, and she was there, in what had become her usual spot at the poker table. She smiled when she saw him, puckered her lips, and continued playing her hand. Carter returned her smile and headed for the office to talk to Knuckles and Kelsey. But before he made it to the office, Kelsey came out.

"What's up, Skipper?"

"Hey, Kelsey," he said to her, but he hadn't turned away from Gianna.

"You find anything else about her?"

"About who?"

"The mystery woman there," Kelsey said and motioned toward Gianna with her head. "You know, the one you haven't been able to take your eyes off since the first time you saw her."

Carter glanced over at Kelsey. "Am I that obvious?"

"Obvious? No." Kelsey laughed. "But anyone who's paying attention could tell that it's obvious that you're digging her."

Although she wasn't ready to accept it, Gianna found herself feeling for Carter the way he was feeling for her. And for her, it couldn't have come at a worse time. She was on a mission, and it did not include falling in love with someone she had met a few days ago and had sex with once.

But it was so good, she thought, and placed her bet. "I raise you twenty," she said and pushed her chips forward. *Or was it because I hadn't had sex with a man in years?*

And it was so very good, she thought, watching Carter and digging the way he moved.

In the same way that Gianna had intrigued him, she was intrigued by Carter. Everything about him made her want to know more.

But that is not *what you're here for,* Gianna told herself. *You need to do what you came to do and move on,* was what she told herself repeatedly, but her curiosity had gotten the better of her.

That was when she saw Aimee Pearce on her way to the ladies' room earlier that evening. She had been trying to strike up a conversation with Gianna since she started coming there. But since she was not looking to make new friends, Gianna was less than cordial.

Besides, she's a little too chatty for my taste, Gianna thought.

But now she needed information.

And who better than Chatty Cathy?

She followed Aimee to the ladies' room and struck up the conversation Pearce had been so anxious to have.

"You come here a lot, don't you?" Gianna asked as the women washed their hands.

Pearce giggled. "I guess you can say I'm a regular. Why do you ask?"

"What can you tell me about Carter Garrison?"

"You mean your hero?" Pearce giggled.

"Yes, my hero." The sound of Pearce giggling annoyed Gianna, and it showed on her face. "Does he own this place?"

"Carter? No. This is Mike Black's spot."

Gianna pointed at Pearce. "Now, *him* I've heard of."

Not only had she heard of him, but Gianna had also actually met Mike Black a time or two back in the day. But that was years ago, and *I was a different person in those days.* Gianna giggled to herself.

"Carter is one of the captains in The Family."

"Is he really?"

So, now she was even more intrigued. Gianna went and reclaimed her seat at the table. For the next hour or so, she played poker and tried to stay on mission. She won some hands, and she lost some hands, but that didn't matter. It wasn't why she was there, but now, it seemed that she had a new purpose in being there. The question was . . . What was she going to do about it?

Gianna glanced at her watch. "That does it for me tonight," she said and stacked her chips.

She looked at Carter. Coincidentally, he was looking at her. Staring, if he wanted to be honest about it. The truth was, he couldn't look away. She motioned with her finger for him to come to her.

"Hello, Carter."

"How are you tonight, Gianna?"

"I'm fantastic." She pointed to her chips. "You wouldn't mind escorting a lady to the cage so she can cash out, would you?"

"It would be my pleasure."

When Carter extended his hand, Gianna handed him her chips. She stood up and looped her arm in his as they walked to the cage.

"Do you have any plans for the rest of your night?"

"I wouldn't mind going somewhere to listen to good music and grab a bite to eat."

"Do you like jazz vocals?" Carter asked.

"It depends on the era, but yes, I do."

"I know a place," Carter said, and he took Gianna to La Chat.

When they arrived there, they were seated at the table Mercedes had reserved for preferred clientele, or those rare occasions when Black and Shy walked in.

Which, by the way, they rarely did.

They had just been served balsamic-glazed steak rolls and Mediterranean shrimp kabobs when Luke McCann, who had started in The Family working security at Cynt's, saw four white men come into La Chat. He immediately got a bad feeling about them. And with good reason. They were members of the Montanari Family.

They were there at La Chat hunting for Shayla Clark, a numbers runner and loan shark who worked for RJ. They were looking for her because she murdered Giovanni

Folliero, a made man in the Montanari Family. He had killed Shayla's brother, Marchello Clark, a gambler and enforcer who worked for Judah.

Knowing that the death of a made man was not going to go unanswered and not wanting to get into another shooting war, Rain had been hiding Shayla at one of her safe houses.

Luke walked over and pointed them out to Mercedes. "Guess you need to find out what the gentlemen want," she said. He approached the men.

"Can I help you, gentlemen?"

"We're looking for Shayla Clark. Where is she?"

"I've never heard of anybody by that name."

"Is that right?"

One of the other men quickly took out a gun and fired at the bottles behind the bar.

"Heard of her now?" the man asked and punched Luke in the face.

The other men picked up chairs and broke them over the tables while the one continued firing at the bar.

Carter took out his gun and stood up. "Wait here."

Then he turned over the table. Gianna got behind the overturned table and reached into her clutch, taking out her SIG Sauer P365 9 mm and making sure that one was in the chamber, just in case shit got wild, and she had to protect herself.

Mercedes reached into her thigh holster, pulled out her Glock 43X, and fired at the shooter. When he returned her fire, Carter aimed and hit him with two shots to the chest. He fell over a table.

The other men opened fire as they retreated. Mercedes shot one in the back as he ran out of La Chat. His men came back for him and dragged him out of there as they fired.

Chapter Twenty-six

When the shooting stopped, Veronica Rose and the band wasted no time and began playing a Chet Baker tune, "Let's Get Lost."

"Well, that was something," Veronica said. "What do you say we get lost in some music, shall we?"

Mercedes settled the crowd with free drinks and a few comp meals for their clientele. Carter rushed to check on Gianna. She saw him coming and put away her gun before he got there.

"Are you all right?" he asked with his hand extended to help her get up from the floor.

"I'm good."

He looked around for Luke. He was talking to Mercedes. "I'll be right back."

"I'm not going anywhere," Gianna said as Carter walked over to where they were talking.

"What was that about?" he demanded to know.

"They said they were looking for somebody named Shayla Clark," a confused-looking Luke informed him.

Carter dropped his head and shook it. "Montanaris."

"Who is Shayla Clark?" Mercedes asked.

"One of RJ's people," Carter said, walking away. He took out his phone and made a call.

"This Rain."

"It's Carter. I'm at La Chat, and we just had four uninvited guests here asking for Shayla Clark. We'll talk about how we left it when I see you."

"Understood," Rain said as she got another call coming through. She looked at the display, "This is her calling now. I'll get with you later." She switched over. "This Rain."

"It's Shayla. Four white men are here, and they're trying to get into the house."

"Montanaris. How did they find you?" Rain questioned.

"I don't know," Shayla lied. She knew exactly how they found her.

Earlier that day, Shayla remembered that one of her clients had a $50,000 loan that was due, and she went to collect.

"Get in the panic room. I'll be there in five minutes," Rain promised.

"Okay," Shayla said, and Rain ended the call.

"What's up?" Alwan asked.

"Take me to the safe house. Montanaris hit La Chat, and they're at the house now."

"How did they find her?" Alwan asked as he made a U-turn and headed for the safe house.

"I don't know. Let's just get there."

"Right."

When they arrived at the house, everything appeared to be quiet. Rain and Alwan drew their weapons and went inside. They moved carefully through the house, checking each of the rooms on that level before going upstairs to the panic room.

Alwan checked the rest of the floor. "Nobody is here, Rain," he reported, and she entered the combination to gain access to the panic room.

"Are you all right?" she asked Shayla.

"I'm fine."

"What happened?" Rain asked.

"Once they searched the house and didn't find me or anything else, the four of them left."

"How did they find you?"

"I don't know," Shayla lied again.

"Doesn't matter. We need to move you—now. Come on."

"What about my stuff?" Shayla asked.

"I'll send someone for it. Right now, we gotta go. Come on. We need to leave," Rain said as she exited the panic room.

"Okay," Shayla said.

She came out of the panic room and followed Rain and Alwan downstairs and out of the house. As soon as Alwan stepped outside, the four members of the Montanaris opened fire from across the street. One of their first shots hit Alwan in the shoulder. He went down.

Rain and Shayla returned their fire, and then they rushed to Alwan, dragging him to cover.

"I'm all right," he said as he struggled to his feet. He took out his gun.

"We gotta get to the car," Rain shouted over the sounds of gunfire. "Let's go!"

All three emerged from their cover position and opened fire as they ran toward their vehicle. Once Rain got Alwan in the backseat, she got behind the wheel. Shayla fired off a few shots before she got in the car, and Rain drove away. The Montanaris quickly got in their vehicle and followed them away from the safe house. When another car of Montanaris joined the pursuit, Rain took out her phone and made a call to Jackie. But Travis was back in the city, so Jackie and Fiona were busy and didn't answer.

"Shit!"

Her next call was to Monika.

"What's up, Sunshine?"

"I got two cars filled with Montanaris on my ass. Where are you?"

"I'm at Honey's. Lead them this way. I'll be ready for you," Monika promised the boss of The Family.

"On my way!" Rain shouted and ended the call.

One of the Montanari cars pulled up alongside them and began firing at the windows with an automatic weapon. Shayla's hands flew to her head, and she ducked, but she was surprised when the onslaught of bullets seemed to bounce harmlessly off the vehicle. Shayla looked over at Rain as she drove.

"The glass is bullet-resistant, and the car is made with reinforced steel."

"Bulletproof?"

"No. Eventually, those shots *are* going to weaken that glass."

"What happens then?"

"We're fucked," Rain said as they approached Honey's. She took out her phone and called Monika again.

"Where are you, Sunshine?"

"I'm close."

"Drive around the block when you get here. We are set up to receive your guests."

"I'm coming."

When Rain got to Honey's gambling spot, she called Monika again.

"We're here. Get ready," Rain said as she turned onto the street around the corner from Honey's.

"We're ready, Sunshine," Monika said and ended the call. "Here they come," she informed her team.

Monika had set up a trap for the pursuing Montanaris. She set up a choke point for them. Therefore, when Rain drove down the street, an SUV pulled out and blocked the street. The Montanari driver slammed on his brakes to avoid hitting the SUV. The car behind them had to slam on its brakes as well. When they did, another SUV pulled out and blocked the street to prevent their exit. Monika, Nick, Xavier, and Honey's men opened fire.

As Shayla joined the firefight, Rain ran to the trunk of her car and took out the SIG Sauer MG338 machine gun that she recently purchased. She'd been looking for an excuse to try it out, and then she ran to get into the action. As she was approaching, it was the first time that she saw Nick. She went and stood next to him as he continued firing at the Montanaris.

Rain blanketed the area with the MG 338 machine gun. Her first volley took out two of the men. Then she dropped for cover and looked at Nick.

"You just don't know how badly I wanna fuck you right now," Rain said, and then she continued firing at the Montanaris.

Nick looked over at Rain as she fired away. Memories of the way that they used to be together came rushing back.

"You don't know how badly I want you to fuck me right now," he said as he rose to his feet and took out another of their Montanari attackers.

The firefight continued, but the Montanaris were outgunned. Within minutes, all eight men were dead. Now that the shooting was over, Honey's men returned to their cars and went back to the club.

Once they were back at Honey's, Rain told Shayla and Alwan that she'd be right back and approached Nick.

"Thank you for coming," Rain said, looking up into Nick's intense eyes and thinking about the old days when he used to fuck the shit out of her and what she said to him during the heat of battle.

"No worries." He stepped a little closer to her. "Glad we could help."

"Look, about what I said . . ." Rain glanced over at her car, and she knew that she had to go and see about Alwan and get Shayla somewhere safe.

"Don't worry about it . . . It was—" he began, but Rain cut him off.

"I'm sorry, but I meant what I said."

Nick stepped a little closer to her. "I meant what I said too."

Rain nodded. She wanted to drag him to the first dark stop she could find and bend her body over so that he could fuck her brains out as he had many times in the past.

"Really?" she questioned.

Nick nodded slowly. "Really."

"Listen, I need to see about Alwan and get Shayla someplace safe right now."

"I understand."

"But I will call you soon," she promised.

"Go handle your business. We'll deal with the question of you and me another time."

Rain started to walk away, but she didn't get far before she turned around and walked back up to Nick.

"Where's your wife?"

"I don't know."

Rain looked at him like he was stupid. "Fuck you mean, you don't know where your wife is?"

"I mean, she's on special assignment for the Colonel, so I have no idea where in the world she is."

"Right." Rain nodded. "I'll call you soon."

"I'll be waiting," Nick said, and then he watched Rain walk away and get into her car.

When she drove off, Monika approached Nick, shaking her head. He could tell by the look on her face that she had something to say, and honestly, he really didn't want to hear it.

"What?"

"I hope you know what you're doing."

"What are you talking about?"

Monika tipped her head to one side and put her hands on her hips. "You and Sunshine." She pointed at Rain's car as she drove away from the ambush. "*That's* what I'm talking about."

"I don't know what you're talking about," Nick said and watched Rain's car until it was out of sight before he turned and faced Monika.

"Really, Nick? *That's* it? You don't know what I'm talking about? Is *that* what you're trying to get me to believe?"

"I don't know what you're talking about."

Monika shook her head and gave him a very disappointed look. "I didn't just meet the two of you. I've known you both for a long time." She poked him in the chest. "And I can read *your* body language. Like I said, I hope you know what you're doing," she repeated and walked away, shaking her head.

"I hope so too," Nick said softly and walked back to his car behind Monika.

Chapter Twenty-seven

It was after four in the morning when Black and Shy arrived in Nassau at Lynden Pindling International Airport. As soon as they were off the plane and passed through customs, Black began making arrangements to take them to Paraíso to share what they had learned with Jada. However, Shy had other ideas.

"I gotta be honest with you, Michael. I'm not in the mood for Jada tonight," she said, and Black chuckled.

"No problem. We can just go to the hotel."

"Good. Jada is easier to take after a good night's sleep," Shy said, and they got in the transportation Black had arranged.

"Change of plan. Take us to The Island House, please," Black told the driver.

It was just after ten that morning when Shy was awakened by a sound that she didn't want to hear.

"Oh no," she sat up in bed and said when Black's satellite phone began ringing. Shy knew that it was either Rain or Monika calling with bad news.

"Oh shit," Black said when he heard it. "What is it now?"

"Nothing good, I can promise you that," Shy said as he got out of bed to answer the phone.

"Hello," he answered.

"It's Rain."

"What's wrong?"

"You still in Nassau?"

"Yes. What's wrong?"

"When are you coming back?"

"I don't know. What's wrong, Rain?"

"The Montanaris paid a visit to La Chat and to my safe house last night."

Black exhaled. "I'll be back as soon as we wrap up things here." He paused. "I'll call you when I get back." He ended the call and dropped the satellite phone on the bed. "Damn it."

"What's wrong, Michael?" Shy asked.

"The Montanaris paid a visit to La Chat, and they hit Rain's safe house last night."

Shy shook her head. "That's the last thing we need."

"Tell me about it." Black sat on the edge of the bed. "Let's wrap up whatever this thing with Jada is and get back to the city."

Shy moved closer to Black and put her arm around his shoulder.

"It's gonna be all right."

"I know. I have you."

She kissed him on the cheek, and they sat quietly for a while. She didn't need to say anything. The fact that she was there to support him and have his back meant everything to him. It always has.

"Come on, Michael," Shy said, easing her hand in his and standing up. She led him to the bathroom.

Once they showered and dressed, they got ready to leave. Shy called the front desk and told them that they were checking out and asked if they would send someone for their luggage. Once that was done, they left their suite at The Island House. It was just before noon after they had checked out.

"Can we eat first? It's easier to deal with Jada on a full stomach," Shy said, and they went to have lunch at The Yellowbell on The Island House property.

After stuffing themselves with beef katsu sando, tenderloin in a tonkatsu sauce, and white chocolate cheesecake, Mr. and Mrs. Black were on their way to Paraíso. When they arrived, they were escorted to Jada's office, where Caprice informed them that Jada wasn't there and asked if they would wait.

"She promised that she would not be long," Caprice advised and showed the Blacks into the office. She made cocktails for both of them, and then she left the office. Thirty minutes later, Jada sauntered into the office.

"Sorry to keep you waiting," she said as she came through the door.

"No worries," Black said, and then he looked and saw what she was wearing. "Jada . . . You're wearing pants," he said, referring to the slacks she was wearing. He laughed because he knew of only one reason for her to be in pants. "Who did you just kill?"

"As you know, Mr. Black, I will not tolerate abusing the ladies," Jada said and told them about a German businessman who beat and tied up one of her ladies and left the property.

"I understand."

"So, tell me, what happened in Barbados with Conrad Boyle?"

"He's dead," Black said flatly, and Jada wasn't the least bit surprised. "We found him hog-tied and shot in the back of the head."

"Just like Lewis Huber," Shy added.

"Somebody is making a statement," Jada said. "What is going on?"

"I'm not sure. All I can tell you for sure is that Mitchell Wright, who worked for Carter Garrison, Donald Pinkney, who worked in Freeport for Napoleon, Lewis Huber, and Conrad Boyle, who both worked for you, are all dead. I do know that Wright mixed up with a drug dealer named Winston Townson, who worked for Modesto Colbert."

"According to my sources, Mr. Colbert is the leader of the drug organization that has been running their product through the island that I told you about."

"That fits. Whatever they were involved in, it involves drugs."

"I see."

"And on top of that, the Montanaris paid a visit to La Chat and to Rain's safe house last night looking for Shayla Clark."

"The Montanaris are the Italians you're hiding one of Sherman Williams's numbers runners from, am I correct?"

"Sherman retired, so she works for RJ now, but yes, you are correct."

"That seems to be a bit more serious than whatever foolishness that the four amigos were into," Jada offered.

"That's an understatement," Shy added to the conversation.

"True. But I'd still like to know what's going on with them."

"Well," Jada began, "I believe that I know somebody who may be able to provide the answers you seek."

"Who's that?" Black asked.

"Roanna Garcia Santos Martinez."

"Who's that?"

"She's Lewis's girlfriend."

"Okay. Let's go," Black said and was about to stand up.

Jada raised her hand, and he froze. "Perhaps it would be better if you sit this one out, Mr. Black, and allow Shy and me to drop in on her to have a chat."

"Why is that?"

"I don't know if you're aware of this, Mr. Black, but physical presence is quite intimidating. And that is not the vibe I'm going for with this visit."

"Okay. I'll be here when you get back."

"We are going to be awhile."

"Okay, Jada." He turned to Shy. "I'll be at the hotel when you're done."

"Splendid." Jada stood up. "I need to change. I'll just be a minute or two," she said and disappeared into her dressing room.

"You two gonna be all right together?" Black asked.

"Of course, we will. Why wouldn't we?"

Black leaned close to Shy. "Because she never has been your favorite person."

"True. But we'll be fine," Shy said confidently, sure she could rise above what, at times, seemed like Jada's superior attitude. "I know how to behave myself."

A few minutes later, Jada emerged from her dressing room wearing a black Oscar de la Renta sheath dress and her signature Jimmy Choo pumps.

"I'm ready," she announced, and Shy stood up.

"Let's go." She put her arms around Black and kissed him. "I'll call you when we're done."

"Okay," Black said and followed Shy and Jada out of the office, feeling a little left out and just a bit useless.

"So, what's the play here, Jada?" Shy asked as Jada's right-hand man, Johnny, drove them to the home of Lewis Huber and Roanna Garcia.

"We are going to offer our condolences over the death of her beloved husband. In the course of that conversation, I will turn the conversation to what they were involved in."

"Do you think she knows?"

"Oh, I am quite sure of it." Jada paused to explain. "A bit about their relationship dynamic. She is the alpha, and he will do anything for her. I wouldn't be a bit surprised if, not only does she know what they are involved in, but that she was also the catalyst behind it."

"She has that much influence over him?"

"Not influence. More like authority over him."

"I see," Shy said.

"Oh yes, and there will definitely be alcohol involved in this conversation," Jada said, and Shy chuckled. "Anything involving Roanna involves alcohol."

When they arrived at the house, Johnny rang the bell. A red-eyed Roanna Garcia Santos Martinez opened the door.

"What do you want, Johnny?" Roanna barked when she opened the door. It was apparent to Johnny that she had been crying.

"I have Jada West *and* Cassandra Black here to see you."

Roanna looked around Johnny at Jada's limousine. She punched him as hard as she could in the chest.

"Why didn't you call and give me some warning that they were coming?"

Roanna was dressed in her bathrobe with a rag tied around her head, and the place was a mess with empty liquor bottles everywhere.

When Johnny shrugged his shoulders and returned to the car, she slammed the door. The first thing she did was grab a trash bag. Roanna gathered up all the empty liquor bottles and tried to straighten up a bit. Then she snatched the rag off her head on the way to the bedroom to change. When she finally opened the door, Jada and Shy were standing there. Roanna wore a short-sleeved shirt and pants, and her long black hair was flowing off her shoulders.

"Good afternoon, Roanna," Jada said.

"Hey, Jada."

"This is Mrs. Black."

"It's an honor to meet you, Mrs. Black."

"It's good to meet you. It's Shy. I'm sorry for your loss."

"Thank you, Shy. That was nice of you to say. And thank you for coming." She wasn't in the mood for guests, so her first instinct was to get rid of them.

Jada held out her hand, and Johnny handed her a bottle of Rose Island Vodka, a Bahamian-made vodka that Roanna drank.

"We came to offer our condolences," Jada said as she handed Roanna the bottle. "May we come in?"

She took the bottle from Jada and quickly stepped aside. "Please, come in, come in."

"Thank you."

Roanna led them into her living room.

"I want you to know how sorry I was to hear about Lewis. He was a good man. If there's anything that you need, I hope you won't hesitate to reach out and ask."

"Thank you, Jada. That is very kind of you to say," Roanna said as Jada and Shy sat down. She held up the bottle. "Can I fix either of you a drink?"

"Certainly not." Jada stood up, straightened her dress, and took the bottle from her. "You relax. I'll take care of it."

"Thank you, Jada."

"Shy," Jada began, and Shy looked at her. "She has rum, but it's Moraga Cay Rum."

"Made right here on the island," Roanna said as Jada handed her a glass full of straight vodka.

"That's fine," Shy said. After Jada poured Shy's drink, she made a French 75 for herself and rejoined Shy and Roanna in the living room.

By the time they finished their third round of drinks, Roanna's lips were flowing, and it was time for Jada to ask what they came there to hear.

"What was Lewis involved in that got him killed, Roanna?" Jada asked as she took her glass to pour another drink.

"We might be able to help," Shy added, trying to sound sympathetic.

"I told him not to do it. That we were doing fine, but he always wanted to do more for me." A tear rolled down her cheek. "I'm the reason he's dead."

"Don't be so hard on yourself." Jada handed her the drink. "Just tell me what happened."

"Lewis told me that he had noticed a weakness in the way some smugglers was doing business, and he could exploit it. I told him it was too dangerous, and he should leave it alone because, like I said, we were doing fine." She shook her head and finished the drink that Jada had just poured for her. Jada stood up quickly and poured herself another drink. "He said it would be easy, and it was too much money to pass up," she cried.

"They robbed the shipment," Shy said flatly, and Roanna took a big swallow and nodded.

"Who was in on the robbery with him?" Jada asked, even though she knew.

"It was Lewis, Conrad, Pink, and some guy from New York named Mitch. They thought they got away with it. For months after that, it was quiet, and then we heard that Pink was dead. Lewis knew he was next." Roanna paused, and a concerned look washed across her face. "Conrad—I need to warn Conrad."

"He's dead, Roanna," Jada said.

"Oh." Roanna got up and poured another glass of vodka. "I was so caught up in my own grief that I didn't even think of him." She shot the drink and poured another. Shy looked at Jada. She nodded.

"Well, my dear, I think we've taken up enough of your time," Jada said and stood up.

Shy stood up. "Yes. And I am so sorry for your loss." She hugged Roanna. "If there is anything you need, please let me know. Michael and I are happy to help out in any way we can."

"Thank you so much for saying that, Mrs. Black. You don't know how much that means to me." Roanna turned to Jada. "Thank you so much for coming, Jada."

"Once again, I am so sorry for your loss," Jada said on her way to the door.

Having gotten what they needed, Shy called Black as they drove away from Roanna's house, and he was still in Jada's office waiting when they arrived.

"I think that they are tying up loose ends," Black said.

"What are you going to do?" Jada asked.

"Nothing. Right now. Modesto Colbert is the least of our worries."

Chapter Twenty-eight

"This Rain."

"We're back," Black said when he and Shy returned from the islands. "Meet me at the house."

"What about the captains?"

"Just you. We'll talk to the captains later."

"On my way," Rain said, and Black ended the call.

His next call was to Bobby.

"What's up, Mike?"

"You heard?"

"I'm fine, Mike. How are you? And yeah, I heard."

"Meet me at the house as soon as you can."

"I'm on my way."

"Call Wanda. Ask her if she'd like to join us."

"You know she does. See you when I get there," Bobby said, and Black ended the call.

When Black and Shy got off the jet, Chuck was there waiting, and he drove them to their house. They were surprised when they got there and saw Wanda's car parked in front of the house and her driver standing next to it.

When the Maybach stopped in front of the house, Wanda's driver opened Shy's door before Chuck got out.

"Good morning, Mrs. Black."

"Good morning."

"I'm Trinity, Ms. Moore's new driver," he said and bowed slightly.

"It's a pleasure to meet you, Trinity," Shy said to the tall, dark, and very handsome man who stood before her. Chuck shook his head and opened Black's door.

"Too slow," Black joked with him and went toward the house.

"Good morning, Mr. Black. Ms. Moore is waiting for you in the media room," Trinity said as Black walked past him. Chuck followed Black and Shy to the house.

"Brownnoser," he said to Trinity, and then Chuck went into the home.

After checking on their mother and Mansa, Black and Shy went to the media room where Wanda was waiting.

"Hello, Mike, Shy." She held up her glass. "I hope you don't mind; I fixed myself a drink."

He saw the pitcher of apple martinis on the bar. "Not at all."

He looked at Shy, both thinking that it was a little early in the day.

Cut her some slack; she just lost her husband, Black thought, so he didn't comment.

"Did Bobby tell you what was going on?"

"No, he didn't have to. I already heard. I still have my sources. I don't know the details, but I know the Montanaris are tired of waiting, and they made a play to take her."

"That's more than I know," Black said as the media room door opened and Bobby walked in. He looked at Wanda.

"How'd you get here so quick?"

"I got a stop not far from here," Wanda replied.

"Oh really, where?" Shy asked excitedly.

"On Pelham Road by New Rochelle Harbor. It's just a little two-bedroom, one-bath spot."

"What made you make the move out this way?" Shy asked.

"I didn't want to be in the house. Way too many memories to deal with in that house," Wanda said as she finished her drink. Then she got up to pour another.

"What you drinking?" Bobby asked.

"Apple martini," she said as she poured.

"Too weak." Bobby went behind the bar, got a bottle of Rémy Louis XIII, and poured it. "Mike?"

"Go ahead."

"Captains coming?" Wanda asked.

"No. We're just waiting for Rain. She's on her way. I wanted us to talk and decide what we're gonna do and then tell the captains what we decide."

"Thank you for including me in the decision," Wanda said. "You usually just decide and let me know. It's nice to be in the room again."

"Glad to have you," Black said.

"And I'm glad you two are glad. Now, somebody wanna tell me what's going on? All I heard was that the Montanaris hit us at La Chat last night."

"That's all I know too, Bob. That's why we're waiting for Rain. They hit her safe house too," Black said.

"What exactly happened would be good to know, but we don't have to wait for Rain to talk about what we're gonna do," Bobby said.

"He's right, Mike," Wanda said.

"Okay, let's talk about it. The Montanaris want Shayla Clark. The only question is, are we gonna give her up?"

"I don't know whether I get a vote, but I'm in the room, so I'm gonna speak my mind. I don't think we should give her up," Shy said. "If he had killed my brother, I would have killed him too. Made man or not." She paused. "Is there anybody in here who can honestly say that they would have done any differently?"

"I can't," Black said and chuckled. "I'd empty the streets over everybody in this room."

"Same here," Bobby said.

"That may be true, but it's not the point," Wanda began as there was a knock at the door, and then Rain walked in.

"Sorry, I'm late." Rain sat down beside Wanda and smiled as she leaned close to her. "I met Trinity outside," she whispered. "Where did you find him?"

"Fine-ass men dot com. We'll talk later," Wanda said, and Rain nodded.

"So what happened last night?" Black asked.

"Carter called from La Chat and said that four Montanaris came there looking for Shayla."

"Why La Chat?" Wanda asked.

"I don't know, but I'm thinking that they chose La Chat because it's a softer target. Carter killed one, and Mercedes shot another, but he lived. The others ran. About that same time, Shayla called me and said four of them were in the safe house."

"How did they find her at the safe house?" Black asked.

"I don't know that either, but I got her outta there. Alwan got shot, but he's gonna be fine. Anyway," Rain got up and went to the bar, "two cars followed us from there. I called Nick and Monika. They set up a kill box around the block from Honey's."

"If Nick and Monika were involved, the only question is, how many did you kill?" Black asked.

"Eight, but Edwina cleaned up the scene."

"Well, that's something, but the fact remains that we dropped nine more Montanaris last night," Bobby pointed out.

"What do you think we should do, Bobby?"

"I'm with Shy," Bobby said. "I don't think we should give her up to them."

"Wanda?"

"I'm gonna play devil's advocate here. Suppose we do give her up to them . . ."

"You serious?" Bobby asked.

"Yes, Bobby, I'm serious. Suppose we turn her over to them, then what?"

"We look weak," Black said.

"But we avert a war with the Montanaris. A war we are not prepared to fight," Wanda pointed out.

"That's true too," Rain said. "But I don't think we should give her up either. What message does it send to our people? That we got your back *except* when you fuck with the wrong people?" She shook her head. "I can't accept that."

"But we avoid going to war with the Montanaris. A war we are not prepared to fight," Wanda repeated.

"What do you think, Mike?" Bobby asked.

"Wanda's right, but so are Cassandra and Rain. We avoid going to war, but we send the wrong message to our people and everybody else. It's like we're announcing that we're weak and can't defend our people."

"So, what are you gonna do?" Wanda asked.

"I'm gonna try to talk our way outta this. I'll reach out to Angelo and see if he can arrange a sit-down with us and the Montanaris."

"And if they don't wanna talk?" Rain asked.

"Then we go to the mattresses," Black said. "Any comments? Bobby?"

"I'm in."

"Wanda?"

"I'm in."

"Rain?"

"You ain't even gotta ask."

"Cassandra?"

"I'm with Rain. You ain't even gotta ask me."

"Is she safe?" Wanda asked.

"At your safe house?"

"I say we move her to the house in Big Cross Cay," Wanda said of the house in the East Grand Bahama district.

"That's a good idea. Can I count on you to make that happen?" Black asked.

"I can take care of that," Wanda said.

"Thank you, Wanda," Black said. "Now, there's something else we need to talk about."

"What's that?"

"This business with Mitch Wright."

"What about him?" Bobby asked.

"First off, who is he?" Wanda asked.

"He was muscle for Carter's crew."

"Okay, now, what about him?" Wanda wanted to know.

"One of our dancers saw Mitch in Nassau. Turns out that Mitch, Donald Pinkney, Lewis Huber, and Conrad Boyle—"

"Who are they?" Bobby asked.

"Pinkney works for Napoleon in Freeport; Huber works for Jada in Nassau; and Boyle works for her in Barbados. They robbed a shipment belonging to Modesto Colbert."

Bobby laughed. "I hate to keep asking this, but who the fuck is he?"

"Some low-rent drug dealer. Anyway, long story short, he had all of them killed."

"What are you gonna do about that?" Wanda asked.

"Nothing. Under normal circumstances, I'd be down to wipe these fucks off the face of the earth, but right now, I think we've got enough on our plate."

"I'm with that. We can't fight wars on two fronts," Rain said.

"We're going to have all we can handle with the Montanaris. A war on two fronts would be bad," Wanda said.

"Agreed," Bobby said.

"Rain, call a meeting with the captains tonight at Honey's. They all need to start recruiting new muscle."

"On it."

"We need to reach out to our friends in Florida about weapons," Bobby said.

"Make that happen, Bobby. And, like I said, I'll reach out to Angelo and see if he can arrange a sit-down with Salvatore Marino."

"He the boss of the Montanaris?" Wanda asked.

"Acting," Rain said. "He grabbed power when Marcell De Luca died a couple of months ago."

"How do you know all that, Rain?" Bobby asked.

"When Shayla killed a made man, I made it my business to find out all I could bout them because I knew this day was coming." She looked at Black. "What time you wanna meet the captains?"

"Around ten."

"I'll make it happen."

"I had no doubt," Black said, and now that he had included his business, he went to the bar and poured a glass of Louis XIII.

Later that night at Honey's, one of the gambling spots run by Jackie Washington's crew, RJ was the first to arrive. When Honey took over and renovated her stop, she had a secure meeting place built at Black's request. They usually held the captains' meetings at Conversations, another of Jackie's spots, but that was a well-known fact. And since they were going to war with the Montanaris, this was a good time to begin utilizing it. Never having hosted a captains' meeting before, Honey wasn't sure what was expected of her.

"Should I have catered? I don't know," Honey questioned. But Jackie wasn't answering her phone, and neither was Fiona. That had been happening more often since Travis got back from Africa. Not sure of the correct protocol, Honey called Cuisine and asked them to prepare their standard business meeting buffet and had it sent over.

Therefore, RJ was surprised, to say the least, when he walked into the room and saw a table with ham and cream cheese roll-ups, Italian meatballs, honey chicken skewers, mozzarella and prosciutto pinwheels, mini spinach and artichoke tarts, sweet potato and feta bites, pesto bread bites, mini sliders, cheese balls, and jalapeño poppers. There was enough food there to feed a small army. He got a plate, filled it, and sat down to eat.

Jackie Washington was next to arrive. Her reaction was the same as RJ's, but she too grabbed a plate and commended Honey for showing initiative. When Rain got there, she didn't say anything; she just got a plate.

"What's all this?" Bobby asked when he got there with Black and Wanda, but, like the others, he wasted no time grabbing a plate. The last captains to arrive were Carter and Ryder.

"Now that we're all here," Black began, "I'm sure by now everybody's heard about the Montanaris hitting us at La Chat, of all places, looking for Shayla Carter."

"What you might not know is that they went after her at my safe house that same night," Rain added.

"How did they find your safe house?" Jackie asked.

"I don't know."

"I think I do," RJ said. "One of my people said they saw Shayla at Doc's old spot."

"What was she doing there?" Carter asked.

"Collecting fifty large from what I hear," RJ responded.

"Not a good excuse," Bobby said. "But I understand not letting that money go uncollected." He looked at his son. "You're her captain."

"*Acting* captain," Ryder said.

"Excuse me, Ms. I just made captain my damn self, Ryder," Bobby said.

"Which is why I'm so protective of the title and the responsibility it carries."

"You saying I don't?" RJ asked.

"We don't have time for this nonsense," Rain said to shut it down before it got started. "Bottom line, I need all of you to start recruiting new muscle."

"We're going to the mattress against the Montanaris, aren't we?" Carter questioned.

"Yes," Black said. "Unless we can talk peace with them, but we are not giving her up."

Chapter Twenty-nine

After meeting earlier that day with Rain, Carter spent the day with Geno. He tasked him with recruiting new muscle. With that in progress, Carter made his rounds to his spots to let the operators know what was to come in the near future.

It was after one in the morning when Carter arrived at Knuckles's spot. When he got there, he looked around for Gianna and found her in her usual spot. She blew him a kiss when she saw him and promptly went all in on an inside straight. When she won, Gianna racked up her chips and announced her departure to a chorus of grumbles from the assembled gamblers. Grumbles that quieted when Carter approached the table.

"Well, hello, Mr. Garrison."

"Ms. Mattise." Carter bowed slightly. "You ready to get outta here?" he asked, reaching for her hand.

"I am. But I wanna do something different tonight."

"What did you have in mind?" he asked as he escorted her to cash in her chips.

"I don't know. Surprise me."

Carter thought for a moment or two. "I got just the thing."

"What's that?" Gianna asked.

"You said to surprise you." He leaned close as they walked. "It kind of ruins the surprise if I tell you what the surprise is, don't you think?"

"I do. But can you give me a hint?" Gianna asked playfully, and she left Knuckles's joint with Carter.

An hour or so later, Carter and Gianna arrived in Chinatown at a restaurant run by Triad member Fai Ling. Carter got out and opened the door for Gianna. They walked toward the building, but instead of going inside the restaurant, Carter walked hand in hand with her into the alley. They went down the dimly lit alley until they reached a door. Carter knocked. A panel in the door opened, and a man looked out.

"DiMaggio," Carter said, and the door opened.

Once they were inside, Carter and Gianna walked down a long hallway to a freight elevator. The conductor closed the gate, and they went down. When the gate opened, they got off and walked into a large, open space in an octagonal steel cage in the center of it. Inside the cage, two men were fighting with bare knuckles. The cage was surrounded by screaming, gambling fight fans.

"Bare-knuckle boxing," Gianna said. "I've always wanted to go to one of these."

"You a fight fan?"

"Yes. Back in the day, I used to go to the fights in Atlantic City and Vegas all the time. But I've never been to a no-holds-barred fight before."

"No, this fight is by Marquess of Queensberry rules."

"I've heard that before, but what does it mean?"

"No wrestling moves or hugging allowed."

"What's the difference?"

"In a no-holds-barred fight, you can use your feet. There are no disqualifications or count-outs, weapons and interference are allowed, and the match only ends by submission or a knockout."

"Got it. How do I gamble?"

"Come on," Carter said, and took Gianna around and introduced her to Mingmei Chang, who took their bets.

They'd been there long enough to gamble on and watch three fights. Gianna was enjoying herself, and Carter was enjoying being with her. It made him think about Mileena and Rain. He thought about how he felt about each one. He loved Mileena and had loved her for years. But his relationship with Rain was totally different; the way it started, how it went, and how it ended.

It began on a humbug.

It just kind of happened one night.

But once it began, it was intense.

And then Rain was gone, and there was nothing. Whereas with Mileena, it was a slow, flirtatious burn that she finally gave in to. His relationship with her was a slow, steady groove that lasted until she grew tired of Carter putting The Family ahead of her all the time. And even then, she intended to make Carter appreciate her and want to choose her over The Family. But then Carter got arrested and was locked up.

When he got out, they tried to make a go of it. Carter and Mileena eased back into the slow, steady groove that they had been in before his incarceration. However, as time passed, the same problem occurred. Carter put the needs of The Family before Mileena, and once again, she grew tired of it, and she was gone again. Despite their differences, the ending of each relationship ripped his heart out. And Carter responded to each in the same way.

Find and conquer as much new pussy as possible.

For Carter, it was an effective way not to feel the pain of the breakup, exchanging them for the thrill of the hunt and the feelings of pleasure that you only got in new pussy. It was a short-lived fix to the pain each woman had caused him, but Carter never actually dealt with what he was feeling, preferring instead to mask it and move on until he no longer felt the pain.

Carter glanced at Gianna as she watched the two combatants throw bare-knuckle bombs at each other. Although he had no idea of who she really was, to him, Gianna was a combination of Mileena and Rain. It had only been a couple of days, but in that short span of time, Carter and Gianna had a slow but very intense groove going. There was a voice in his head that was screaming, "*Hey, you better slow down.*" But when he looked into her eyes, that voice was telling him to dive in deeper.

It made him wonder if he found himself feeling for Gianna the way he felt for Mileena and Rain, would it end the same way with her ripping his heart out? He didn't know, so he was doing what felt good to him.

"*Dive in deeper, it will be all right,*" the voice in his head kept saying.

That voice was dominant and silenced the protective voice of reason.

For Gianna, things couldn't be more different. Even though they were each struggling with the same emotions, she was digging the slow but intense groove they were in, but Gianna cursed those feelings and was trying to push them away. She was falling in love with Carter, and that was not what she wanted. Falling in love was not what she needed to be focusing her attention on. Gianna had a purpose, and that, to her, was all that mattered. But now, this was happening, and she felt that she was powerless to stop it.

And then, something happened to bring her purpose back into focus. She saw somebody she knew. His name was Keaton Douglas. He was working as a long-haul trucker now, but back when she knew him, he was a player on the rise in the dope game. However, as Sir Isaac Newton once said, "What goes up must come down."

Well, true to the statement about gravity coming down, Douglas was arrested. Then he began flipping on everybody higher up on the food chain than he was. That was the beginning of the end.

"This place got a ladies' room?" Gianna asked Carter.

"Huh?" Carter, who was deep into the fight, asked.

"Ladies' room. Where is it?"

Without looking away from the action, Carter pointed in the direction of the restroom before he caught himself. "Come on, I'll show you."

"No. You enjoy the fight," Gianna said, keeping her eyes on Keaton Douglas. "I'm a big girl. I'll be all right going to the bathroom by myself."

"You sure?" Carter asked without looking away from the fight.

"Yes, Carter, I'll be fine."

Once again, Carter pointed in the direction of the bathrooms. "Over there in the corner on your right."

"Thank you, Carter. I'll be right back," Gianna said and followed Douglas.

Gianna walked quickly to catch up with him. When he went into the men's room, she thought she had lost him.

"Shit," she said to herself.

While she waited in the hallway for him to come out, Gianna reached into her clutch and discreetly took out her gun. She put a silencer on it and was standing at the door when he exited.

"Hello, Dougie."

He looked at her strangely. "Do I know you?"

"You used to know me, Dougie. Before you betrayed me."

She raised her gun.

"Akira?" he questioned before she fired a shot that hit him in the forehead. When his body dropped, she shot him twice more in the chest.

Gianna walked away quickly. Taking the silencer off her gun as she walked, she returned it to her clutch. As she left the area, Gianna heard a woman scream. She couldn't be sure if the woman saw her leaving the area, so it was time to get outta there.

Gianna kissed Carter on the cheek. "Miss me?" she asked when she returned.

"I did."

She kissed him on the other cheek. "This was fun, but I wanna get outta here."

"What do you wanna do?"

Gianna looped her arm in his. "Let's go to La Chat. I like the singer," she said as they walked toward the exit. "What was her name again?"

"Veronica Rose."

"Yes. She has such a beautiful voice."

When Carter and Gianna arrived at La Chat, Veronica Rose and her new band, Rooi, were on stage playing her version of Nina Simone's "Feeling Good." They were seated at the reserved table down front, where they indulged in the caviar from Caspian Monarque and Dom Pérignon Vintage 2012 Champagne because Carter said, "Being with you is like a celebration of what's to come."

"Then we should definitely celebrate," Gianna said.

While they enjoyed the music, Gianna looked at Carter and thought about what she was doing and what she was allowing herself to feel. This was not part of the plan. This was not what she'd invested all this time and money in. But here she was, allowing herself to fall in love with Carter Garrison. Sure, she killed Keaton Douglas, and that was all well and good, but Dougie wasn't even on her list; he was a bonus, and besides, he had it coming. She'd just forgotten his involvement when she made her list of seven.

Gianna took a minute to consider the position she found herself in. Carter Garrison was a captain in Mike Black's criminal organization. She understood what that meant and what it potentially meant to her. Carter Garrison, aside from being handsome and fucking her like she hadn't been fucked before, carried power, *real* power. She could forgo her revenge and settle into life as his woman and be happy.

She laughed to herself because, before now, happiness wasn't even a consideration. It wasn't even about taking back what was once hers. She had decided that was behind her. All she had to look forward to was seeing each of those who betrayed her dead. Of the seven, four were dead. The last three names on her list were proving more challenging.

"What are you thinking about?" Carter leaned over and whispered in her ear.

The question caught her off guard. She paused to think before she answered. "I was thinking about the future and what it could look like," she said.

"What does the future look like?"

"I don't know yet."

"What do you want it to be?"

Gianna let out a little laugh. "That's what I'm trying to figure out."

"Can I help?"

"No," Gianna said flatly. "You're what I'm trying to figure out."

"Is that a good thing or a bad thing?"

"I don't know yet. That's what I'm trying to figure out."

Carter laughed. "I'm not so hard to figure out."

"You're not?"

"No, I'm not."

Gianna leaned forward and folded her hands in front of her. She smiled.

"Please, enlighten me, Mr. Garrison."

"Sure." Carter sipped his drink. "I'm the type of person who knows what's important to him."

"What's important to you?"

"My Family."

"That it?"

"I'm not gonna lie or pretend, not with you. For the most part, yes. Nothing comes before my responsibility to my Family."

"Mike Black's Family."

"What do you know about that?"

"Not much, really. Just what I've heard over the years."

"And that is?"

"That Mike Black is not a fan of drugs or drug dealers."

"True."

"I have two questions."

"That's odd."

"What's odd?"

"You, having a question." Carter took a sip of his drink and leaned toward Gianna. "Since I met you, you haven't asked me a single question."

"And you haven't asked me any either."

"No. No, I haven't."

"Why is that?"

"I'm relaxing and enjoying the you that you want me to know." Carter paused to see what she would say. "When you want me to know more, you'll show me more."

Gianna said nothing for a while and thought about the future she had just pictured, Carter Garrison's woman, and thought about telling the truth about who she is or was. But that was when Veronica Rose broke into Eddie Cooley and John Davenport's "Fever."

Carter reached for her hand. "Let's dance."

"I love this song."

While they were dancing, Gianna whispered, "You give me fever when you kiss me. Fever when you hold me tight. Fever in the morning. Fever all through the night."

"You're my flame," Carter said, quoting another line from the song.

While they were dancing, she allowed herself to get caught up in the future with Carter that she pictured. But all the while, she knew that tomorrow, this good feeling would pass, and she'd be back on the hunt for her prey. When the last three were dead, then, and only then, could she give herself totally to this future.

Chapter Thirty

In the days that followed, Black reached out to Angelo about arranging a sit-down with Salvatore Marino, the boss of the Montanari Family. While he waited for a response, The Family prepared to go to war.

Carter spent a good part of the day at Purple Rock with Rain and the other captains. While others took on the responsibility of recruiting new soldiers to fight the war, Rain and the captains focused on the safety and security of their operation and the people who worked for them.

"Everybody in this Family ain't a gangster. We need to make sure that none of them get caught up in this war, understand?"

"Understood," they all said.

"Carter."

"Present."

"Your job is to keep the money flowing. That means that you make sure that nothing the rest of us are doing to fight this war affects business. You make sure that we are still doing business as usual."

"Got it."

"Because of her experience with the BBKs, for the purposes of fighting this war, Jackie will serve as my wartime consigliere."

"I'll do my best for you," Jackie promised.

"I know you will." Rain turned to RJ and Ryder. "You two new captains," she laughed. "Our job is to fight the war. Once they hit us, we won't be waiting around reacting to what they do. We're gonna take it straight to them. Our job is to make them want to scream, 'Peace.'"

"Me and Money been sizing up their operation," RJ said and told Rain and her captains about how and where the Montanaris made their money.

"Can't fight a war without money, so hitting those spots and shutting down their moneymaking operations is where we're gonna focus."

"Using that same logic, can't we expect them to come at us the same way?" Ryder asked.

"You let Carter worry about that. You keep your mind on what you need to do. Do you understand me, New Captain?"

"Yeah, Rain, I understand," Ryder said.

"Good." Rain turned to Carter. "But she's right."

"Understood."

While RJ and Ryder saw to the recruitment efforts, Carter, Jackie, and Rain made the rounds of all the spots in The Family. The last place they went to was Knuckles's place. While they were there, Gianna arrived wearing a Givenchy asymmetric dress and stitched leather sandals with a crystal detail.

Her heart beat a little faster when she saw him, and she found herself getting jealous of the attention that he was paying to Jackie and Rain. She had just taken what had become "her seat" at the poker table when Carter saw her. He found himself speechless when Gianna blew him a kiss.

Carter smiled.

"What you smiling about?" Rain asked.

"Huh?"

"I said, what are you smiling about?"

"I'm in a good mood."

"Why?"

"Because I got a good feeling about what we've done to get ready," he lied and thought about something Black said to him.

"Maybe what you need is something more than just some new pussy. Find one who holds your attention. And she isn't a murderer."

His response was, "Right. Where is she?"

And to that, Black said, "She's around, waiting for you to take her."

He looked at Gianna as she looked at her cards and wondered if she could be that woman. She was definitely holding his attention, but he wondered if the rest of that was true. He knew nothing about Gianna Mattise except for what she had shown him in the few days that they'd shared. The question was, who was she before two years ago, when she became Gianna Mattise, and, at this point, did it matter?

No. No, it doesn't matter, he thought as Rain talked, but he wasn't listening. All he could hear at that moment was Gianna whispering, "You give me fever when you kiss me. Fever when you hold me tight. Fever in the morning. Fever all through the night."

"Carter!" Jackie said to break him out of the trance Gianna had cast over him.

"Huh?"

"We about to get outta here and go to Purple Rock," she said.

"I'm gonna hang out here for a minute. I might come through there later."

Rain laughed. "That'll be a first."

"What do you mean?"

"I mean, you ain't been there since I opened the joint. That's what that means." She laughed. "But I get it. The truth is, I don't want your ass up in there. But you are more than welcome there."

"Thank you, Rain." He bowed slightly. "That's good to know."

"We gone," Jackie said. In addition to serving as Rain's wartime consigliere, Jackie was also functioning as Rain's bodyguard.

Once they were gone, Kelsey placed a glass of Hennessy Paradis in front of Carter and smiled.

"How you doing tonight, Skipper?"

"Doing great, Kelsey. What about you?" he asked her, but he was looking at Gianna as she went all in on her hand.

That was when Gianna saw Philip Parrish walk into Knuckles's joint. He was calling himself Damien Kaufman these days. He may be calling himself Damien Kaufman, but he still had Philip Parrish's habits that he liked to indulge in occasionally. One of those was gambling at Knuckles's spot. The people there still called him Parrish.

Back in the days when he was Philip Parrish, a wiretap investigation revealed that Parrish conspired with others to possess, sell, and distribute narcotics obtained from sources in Puerto Rico. Parrish then conducted a series of sales with an undercover officer and was arrested and charged with the sale of a controlled substance in the first and second degrees. He was offered protective custody in exchange for his testimony; all he needed was somebody to flip on.

Gianna had been hunting Parrish for weeks when she heard that he still gambled there sometimes, and she had been coming there every night, waiting for him to show. She planned to watch him and wait until he left Knuckles's spot. Then she would follow and kill him.

She sat there watching him and remembered hearing of his arrest and thinking that he was a stand-up guy who she could depend on. Therefore, she got him a lawyer. When Parrish quickly fired the lawyer, everybody got worried. But nobody expected him to flip and testify against everybody. That was the beginning of her downfall.

The more Gianna thought about it, the angrier she got.

Gianna reached into her leather clutch and took out her SIG Sauer P365 9 mm. Once she made sure that one was in the chamber, she stood up and, without saying another word, walked up to Parrish.

"Payback time, Phil," she said before she shot him in the head. Then she stood over him and shot him twice in the chest.

Carter and all Knuckles's people took out their guns.

"What the fuck?" he questioned, pointing his gun at Gianna.

She held up her hands. "I can explain." Gianna put down her gun.

Carter held up his hand and waved off his men. "I'll take care of this," Kelsey said, pointing to the body. She signaled for her men, and they quickly removed the body.

"You." Carter pointed his gun at Gianna. "You're with me," he said and turned toward the office.

Knuckles put his gun in Gianna's back. "Move," he said and shoved her forward.

Chapter Thirty-one

With her hands still raised, Gianna walked to the office with Carter and Knuckles. She hoped that the relationship she had developed with Carter would be enough to get her out of whatever was to come once she reached the office. She knew that she now needed, for more reasons than just the murder of Philip Parrish, to tell Carter the truth.

"I got her," Carter said to Knuckles when they reached the office.

"You sure, Skipper?" Knuckles asked because he wanted to hang around and hear what Gianna had to say regarding what she had done.

"Yeah," Carter said, looking at Gianna with his gun still pointed at her. "I'm sure," he said, and Knuckles left.

When the door closed, Carter lowered his gun a little and, once again, thought about what Black said to him.

"Find one who holds your attention. And she isn't a murderer."

So much for that, Carter thought.

"What the fuck, Gianna?"

"I can explain."

"I'm listening."

"Can I put my hands down?" she asked

Carter nodded. "Go ahead."

"Thank you." Gianna pointed to one of the chairs in front of the desk. "May I sit?" she asked, and once again, Carter nodded. "Thank you."

Gianna sat down and looked into Carter's eyes, hoping to find some sign of compassion. She found none. What she saw was his understandable anger.

"I was betrayed by some of my people," she began.

Carter nodded and went to sit behind Knuckles's desk. He kept his gun pointed at her.

"Go on."

"I was sentenced to thirty years on racketeering charges, witness tampering, money laundering, five counts of conspiracy to murder, and the murders of Kenrick Tugwell, Nate Tilden, Brian MacDonnell, and Silvino Casarz, and obstruction of justice."

She paused to see if Carter would say anything. When he neither commented nor lowered his gun, she continued.

"The man I killed, his name is Philip Parrish."

"I know who he was. Why'd you kill him?"

"Because he was one of the men who testified against me. His testimony started a domino effect that led right to me. People that I knew for years, people I thought I could trust, all of them testified against me. There were seven of them." Gianna paused. "Well, eight," she added when she thought about the murder of Keaton Douglas.

"Were?" Carter questioned.

"Six of the men who betrayed me are dead now. I killed them."

"What about the other two?"

"Adam Gatewood and the man I thought was my right-hand man, Modesto Colbert."

When Gianna said that Modesto was one of the men who had betrayed her, Carter remembered what Marvin said when he was asked about Winston Townson.

He took over that crew when Modesto Colbert flipped on Akira Dennison and got her sent to prison.

"He was allowed to plead guilty to some fuckin' misdemeanor charge of criminal possession in the seventh degree of a controlled substance, so the bastard testified against me and took over my operation."

"Damn," Carter said. He stood up and went to the bar in the office. He picked up a bottle of Hennessy Paradis and held it up. "You want one?"

"Thank you," Gianna said as she stood up and came to the bar.

Carter poured them both drinks and handed one to Gianna. The fact that he offered her a drink instead of shooting her made Gianna feel better about the situation. But she knew that she wasn't out of the woods yet because, although it wasn't pointed at her, Carter still had his gun out.

"Thank you." Gianna drank her drink in one swallow.

"Go on," Carter encouraged, puring her another.

"I served five years in prison at Bedford Hills Correctional Facility for Women before I was able to escape."

"How did you escape?"

"It was me and two other women, Miriam Hale and Cara Berger." She paused. "Mitzi was fuckin' the prison dentist. She got him to smuggle in diamond-tipped cutting equipment that we used to cut through the bars. Then we made our way through plumbing tunnels and then used bedsheets to rappel down the wall."

"What happened to them?"

"They went right back to their people and got arrested within a week and taken back to prison."

"How did you get away?"

"I was able to get out of the country and made it to Colombia. I had some connections there and access to the money I'd been banking there for years." Gianna shot her drink, and he poured her another. "I was set. I got an apartment at the Amalfi Tower in Cartagena." She giggled. "I even got a piece of a job."

"What were you doing?"

"English-speaking tours of Isla del Pirata Resort."

"What happened?"

"After a year in exile, I got restless living the good, quiet life and started thinking about revenge against the people who betrayed me. I knew somebody who turned me on to one of the best plastic surgeons in Buenos Aires, Dr. Andres Cotillarda."

"I was going to ask you why Parrish didn't recognize you."

"Plastic surgery." She paused. "Otherwise, I couldn't just walk up to Parrish and kill him."

"No, I guess you couldn't."

"That's my story."

"So, what's your real name?"

"If it's all the same to you, I'd rather not say."

"I understand. What's next?"

"I hunt down the next name on my list."

"If you don't mind me asking, who is that?"

"Adam Gatewood."

"What did he do?"

"He testified that I ordered him to kill Jodey MacSwain."

"Did you?" Carter asked.

"Did I what? Order Adam to kill MacSwain?"

"Yeah."

"Yes." Gianna smiled. "I was guilty as sin."

Carter chuckled. "Who's MacSwain?"

"He used to run my heroin business. I lured him to the office at Club 47."

"I remember that place. I used to go there before I got locked up."

"It was the place to be back in the day. Anyway, when MacSwain showed up in Gatewood's office for the meeting, I told him to make himself comfortable and asked Adam to get MacSwain a drink. But instead of getting the drink, Adam took out a 9 mm with a silencer from a cabinet behind MacSwain and shot him in the back of the head."

"You know where to find him?"

"I don't. But I know his habits. He won't be hard to hunt down."

"Only one thing I can do."

"What's that?"

"Help you."

"Why would you do that?"

"I have my reasons," Carter said, knowing that if he were going to do that, he would need to talk to Rain first.

Chapter Thirty-two

Carter and Gianna spent the night at the Residence Inn at Metro Center Atrium in the Bronx. The following morning, when Carter woke up, he took a quick shower and got dressed. While dressing, Gianna woke up.

"Where are you going so early?" she asked because it wasn't ten o'clock yet.

"There are some people that I need to talk to," he said, hating the fact that, according to the chain of command, it was Rain whom he needed to speak to about this. He had been chastised by both Black and Rain the last time he did that, and he had no intention of doing it again, even if that meant telling his old woman about his new woman.

"About me?"

"Yes."

"I wanna go."

Oh, hell no, Carter thought. "Not gonna happen."

"Why not? You're going to talk about me," Gianna said and rolled over. "I think I need to be there."

Carter laughed out loud. "Like I said, not gonna happen," he replied, and once he was dressed, he headed toward the door. "If you're not here when I get back, I'll understand," he said and left the room. Carter closed the door and leaned against it for a while before he headed toward the elevator.

Once he was out of the building and in his car, he took out his phone to call Rain.

"This Rain."

"I need to talk to you. Where you at?"

"I'm about to go through the gate at Black's house."

"I'm on my way out there," Carter said and ended the call.

The fact that she was at Black's house made him feel a little better about the conversation that he needed to have, but he knew that even though it was over between them, Rain wouldn't take the news that he was fucking Gianna well.

When Rain arrived at the house, Roland waved her in before he returned to the gatehouse and picked up the phone to call Black.

"Yes, Roland?"

"Ms. Robinson just came through the gate, Boss."

"Thank you," Black said and ended the call.

He was outside at the pool with Michelle. They had both swum their laps for the day and were talking about the business that she was doing with Barbara.

"Rain's here."

"Can I stay?" Michelle asked and gritted her teeth as she awaited his answer.

"Do you still think you have to ask?"

Michelle smiled. "I guess I still do."

"You are welcome to stay, but you know the rules."

"Keep my mouth shut and listen."

"Yes." Black paused. "One day, all of this is gonna be yours to command. I need you to know everything."

"Yes, Daddy."

"Now, go put something on."

"Yes, Daddy," Michelle said and stood up. She put on the Givenchy lace cover-up and sat down again to await the arrival of the boss of The Family.

Black shook his head because the cover-up was lace and actually left little to the imagination, but it was just Rain, so it was no big deal.

When Rain entered the house, Chuck told her that Black and Michelle were outside at the pool. However, before she went to the pool, Rain stopped in the kitchen to speak to Black's mother. When she burst through the kitchen door, both of the Golden Girls were in there.

"Hey, Rain," Joanne said.

"Good morning, Ms. Sims. Hey, Ms. Black."

"Good morning, Lorraine. Have you eaten breakfast yet?"

"No, ma'am," Rain said. She was hungry, which is why she stopped in the kitchen first. She sat down at her place at the table.

"I have some food left over from Michael and Michelle," M said and got up from the table. "But I'll make something fresh for you."

"You don't have to do that, Ms. Black," Rain said, and Joanne laughed.

"Yes, she does, Lorraine. She cooks; therefore, she is," Joanne said.

It was thirty minutes later when Black's phone rang again.

"Yes, Roland?"

"Mr. Garrison is here."

"Tell him that we're at the pool."

"Yes, Boss," Roland said and relayed the message to Carter.

When he arrived at the house, instead of ringing the bell, Carter went around the home to the pool. Michelle stood up when she saw him come through the gate.

"Good morning, Mr. Garrison," Michelle said, and she shook hands with Carter.

"Morning, Michelle, Mike."

"Please, have a seat," Michelle said.

"Thank you." Carter sat down. "I was supposed to be meeting Rain here. I saw her car, so I know she's here."

"Probably got sidetracked by my grandmothers. She's likely in the kitchen," Michelle said and stood up. "I'll go get her," she said as Rain came out of the house.

"Sorry to keep y'all waiting," Rain said as she approached the others and sat down. "What's up?"

"Tell me, what's going on with us beefing up?" Black said.

"If we gotta go to the mattress, we'll be ready to fight off the Montanaris," Rain said, and then she looked at Carter. "What did you wanna see me about?"

"About a month ago, a woman calling herself Gianna Matisse started coming to Knuckles's joint with Kamari Andrews. Kelsey checked her out and couldn't find anything on her beyond two years ago, so I had Carla and Monika check her out, and they found the same thing. Nothing past two years ago. Last night, she killed one of Knuckles's regulars."

"What was his name?" Rain asked.

"Philip Parrish."

"I know Parrish. Why'd she kill him?" Rain asked.

"She said that him and six other people testified against her. One of them is Modesto Colbert."

"Akira Dennison," Black said.

"She will neither confirm nor deny that she is Akira Dennison," Carter said.

"I thought she was still in prison," Black stated.

"She escaped, and now she's going after everybody who testified against her. There are two more people on her list. Colbert and a guy named Adam Gatewood."

Rain laughed. "Like she's doing us a favor, taking care of Colbert."

"I agree," Black said. "Our priority remains the Montanaris."

"I agree," Rain cosigned.

"Keep doing what you're doing, but keep me posted," Black requested.

"You got it, Mike."

"Anything else?" Black asked, and Carter shook his head.

"That's all I got," Rain said and stood up. When she did, Carter stood up too, and they left the pool together.

"What did you think?" Black asked Michelle once they were gone.

"First, who is Modesto Colbert?"

"You remember, he's the drug dealer Carter told us about."

"I do remember now. You told Mr. Garrison to talk to Jackie about hitting Winston Townson." Michelle nodded. "Go on."

"Mitch was involved with three of our people, and they ripped off one of their shipments. In retaliation, they killed four of them. I decided that we gotta go to war with the Montanaris; it's our priority, not Colbert."

"This woman killing Colbert would be doing us a favor," Michelle acknowledged.

"Right."

"I do have a question for you."

"What's that?"

"The war with the Montanaris."

"What about it?"

"I keep thinking that the needs of the many outweigh the needs of the few or the one."

"No, you didn't just quote Spock."

"Yes, I did. And I think it's a valid point. Do the needs of the many outweigh the needs of the few or the one?"

"Ask your question."

"Is Shayla Clark worth it?"

"As a simple math problem, no."

"Then why are we even considering going to war?"

"Because it's not a math problem. It's a question of loyalty regarding our people."

"I get that, I do, but the question still stands. Is she worth the life of those who will die to protect her while she sits comfortably in Aunt Wanda's safe house in Big Cross Cay?"

"No."

"Then why are we doing it?"

"What would you do?"

"As a matter of principle, I would probably do the same thing you're doing."

Black nodded. "I see your point, though. And that is why I wanna talk first. Remember, diplomacy before war."

"Yes, Daddy."

"Naturally, my preference would be to resolve this without any more bodies dropping. But I also know that we need to be ready in case they come at us again."

"You think they will?"

"I don't know. If Carter hadn't been at La Chat that night, things would have gone differently. They picked La Chat because it's a soft target."

"Right," Michelle agreed. "Since we stopped the prostitution running out of there, other than Cuisine, it is the softest target."

"I'm glad you agree."

"In principle." Michelle nodded and smiled. "I'm glad that it's not my call to make."

"Now it is."

"What?"

"It is your call to make."

"What do you mean it's my call to make?"

"I mean, I am going to make every attempt to resolve this diplomatically. I reached out to Angelo to arrange a sit-down with me and Salvatore Marino, the boss of the Montanari Family. But if I can't come to an understanding, if they wanna go to war over this, then it's your call whether we give her up to avoid war."

Chapter Thirty-three

It was getting late in the afternoon, and Carmen and her team—producer Lacara Krisella, Stephanie Zaire, who maintains her blog, researchers Anisa Rodriguez and Willie Russell, and reporter Darcie Roman—were wrapping up a production meeting for *Carmen Taylor Reports,* the monthly news magazine that Carmen hosted.

That month's show focused on the death of Solomon Fuentes, who was shot thirty-seven times after he pulled out a knife and threatened to harm himself and the police. Witnesses reported that police officers responded and attempted to get Fuentes to put down the knife. When Fuentes refused to drop it and eventually advanced toward the police, he was shot to death.

"Does anybody have anything else before we wrap up?" Carmen asked.

"Not about Fuentes," Anisa said.

"What you got?"

"It's about Patsy McWalter."

"I say again, what you got?" Carmen asked.

"I talked to a woman." Anisa flipped through her notes. "A woman named Alison Everett, who said that Winter told her that she was pregnant, but she wouldn't say who the father was because he was a 'dangerous man,' and she was afraid of him."

"Is she a credible source?" Lacara asked.

"What can you tell me about her?" Carmen asked.

"Well, she's a 24-year-old semiprofessional soccer player. British. Defines herself as straight, currently single, and grew up in a working-class neighborhood. Her mother was an addict, and her father left when she was young. I don't know if that makes her credible or not, but that's who she is."

"How does she know Winter?" Carmen asked.

"She and Winter enjoy photography together."

"How do we substantiate that?"

"Find out who her doctor was," Stephanie suggested.

"And how do you find out who the father was?" Carmen asked.

"Especially when he might be the killer," Lacara said.

"Let's not get too far out on our skis here."

"Unwanted pregnancy is a powerful motive for murder," Anisa added to the discussion.

"All true," Carmen said and paused to think. "So, how do we find out who her doctor was?"

"You could try the direct approach and ask her mother," Willie suggested.

"You think she'll just up and tell you?" Anisa asked. "Please, have you met that walking freezer unit? She's got as much personality as . . ." Anisa paused. "As my refrigerator." She laughed, and the team joined in.

"Still." Carmen raised her hand to calm the laughter. "Elizabeth McWalter is going to be the best source of information."

"If you can get her to open up," Lacara said. "Which you haven't been able to do."

"Yet. I haven't been able to do it yet," Carmen said. "But there's a way to pull it all out of her. I just need to find the trigger, and it will all come rolling out."

"I've always thought she knows more than she's saying," Stephanie said. "I think she knew exactly who her daughter was and is trying to protect the family's reputation."

"At the expense of solving her daughter's murder?" Willie asked skeptically.

"I do," Stephanie said confidently.

"Okay, how do we get her to open up?" Carmen asked. Silence blanketed the room. "Come on, people, I'm open to suggestions here." Carmen waited. "Nothing?" She paused. "You're all fired," she said to a room now filled with laughter. "Thank you, everybody," Carmen said and stood up. "Stephanie, Lacara, stick around for a minute," she requested as the rest of the team filed out of the room.

"What's up?" Lacara asked.

"I agree with Stephanie. Elizabeth McWalter knows more about Winter's murder than she's telling."

"Okay. What do we do about it?" Lacara asked, and Carmen paused to think.

"Stephanie, I want you to review the police reports and compare them with every word Elizabeth and Fredrick have said."

"You think there's something there?" Lacara asked.

"I don't know, but it's a place to start."

"I'll get right on that," Stephanie promised.

"Thank you," Carmen said to end the meeting. Several days later, Stephanie stuck her head in Carmen's office.

"Got a minute?"

"All the time in the world. What you got?"

Stephanie walked in and plopped down into a chair. "I got nothing. I compared the police reports with everything the McWalters have said, either publicly or to you, and I got nothing. They are very careful about what they say." She chuckled. "Which makes me more convinced that I'm right. She found her daughter beaten to death. Where's the emotion?"

"Some people aren't emotional. But I get what you're saying."

"Cry. Have an emotional breakdown on camera—something. But not them. Stone-faced."

Just then, Lacara came into the office and sat down.

"What y'all talking about?"

"Mr. and Mrs. Stone-faced McWalter and the fact that they are dispassionate about their daughter's murder," Stephanie said, and Lacara nodded in agreement.

"So, let's give a chance to show some passion," Carmen suggested.

"What are you talking about?" Lacara wanted to know.

"Just that. Let's give them a chance to show some passion. Stephanie, I want you to call Elizabeth under the pretense of doing a follow-up story to keep the story fresh in the public's mind because the police haven't identified her killer. Then we encourage her to make a more emotional plea to pull at the public's heartstrings."

Lacara nodded. "That actually might work. And it will make for good television if nothing else."

"Once we get her talking, we'll see where she goes."

"I like it," Lacara said. "Make it happen."

Stephanie made the call, and nobody was surprised that Elizabeth McWalter was resistant to the idea. However, once Stephanie put Carmen on the phone with her, she was able to persuade her to do the interview.

"And one more thing, Mrs. McWalter. This may be more effective in getting the public's help if you were to get visibly emotional."

"That's really not me, Ms. Taylor. I tend to keep my emotions to myself."

"Yes. I completely understand. I'm a very private person myself. My father taught me and my sister, as young girls, to keep our emotions to ourselves because people would use that to take advantage of us."

"My father taught us the same thing. Only his warning was specifically about men."

Carmen laughed. “Mine too.”

“Okay, Ms. Taylor. We’ll try it your way,” Elizabeth McWalter agreed now that they had found common ground to stand on.

“Thank you, Mrs. McWalter,” Carmen said and ended the call.

On the day of the interview, Carmen did an emotional and heartfelt interview with Elizabeth McWalter, where she pleaded with the viewers for help in solving her daughter’s murder. She then took it a step further by announcing a reward for information that leads to the arrest and conviction of the responsible party or parties.

“Fifty thousand dollars.”

However, she wasn’t able to steer the conversation toward the name of Winter’s doctor.

“Thank you for watching *Carmen Taylor Reports*. My guest was Elizabeth McWalter, mother of Patsy McWalter, who is just seeking answers. I’m Carmen Taylor.”

“And we’re out,” Lacara said.

“Whew. I could use a drink,” Elizabeth announced.

“I know how you feel,” Carmen said, sensing an opportunity.

“You should join me.”

“Let me get rid of my crew and I will,” Carmen said and went to talk to Lacara.

“She’s drinking with you,” Lacara laughed. “She doesn’t know it yet, but she’s about to tell you her whole life story.”

“I’ll settle for just the name of Winter’s doctor,” Carmen said.

Once the production crew was gone, Elizabeth broke out the bourbon.

“Woodford Reserve, all right?”

“I’m more of a rum runner myself, but I can appreciate a fine Kentucky bourbon,” Carmen replied.

Well, Elizabeth didn't spill her life story, but after her third glass, she did provide Carmen with the information she was seeking. They were talking about how traumatic it must have been to find her daughter beaten and at death's door.

"I believe that I was in shock. I was frozen. I couldn't think straight."

"I can only imagine. And then having to pull it together to call the police."

"I didn't call the police."

"You didn't?"

"Not right away." Elizebeth took a sip. "I called Dr. Ritchie first. He was here in five minutes."

"Really?"

"I thought she might still be alive. But she was gone. Once Dr. Ritchie pronounced her dead, I called the police."

"I see," Carmen said, nodding in understanding, because it explained how calm Elizabeth was when she made the 911 call.

Now that she knew the name of the doctor, Carmen needed to find out if she was, indeed, pregnant.

"How are you gonna do that? There is such a thing as doctor/patient confidentiality," Lacara questioned.

"I have my ways," Carmen said, and she went to talk to Carla. She had no problem hacking the doctor and found that Patsy Winter McWalter was four months pregnant at the time of her death.

"What now?" Lacara asked.

"Now we need to talk to Alison Everett, the woman who told Anisa that Winter was pregnant."

"But she said she didn't know who the father was," Lacara commented.

"But she does know something," Carmen said, and she had Anisa arrange a meeting with Alison Everett. The following day, Carmen met her at The Polo Bar.

"Thank you for taking the time to talk to me, Ms. Everett."

"Alison, and it's no problem. Anything I can do to help them catch Winter's killer, I'm ten toes down for that."

"How did you know that Winter was pregnant?"

"She told me. We were getting high that day. She had just come back from the doctor, and she said that she was pregnant, and she didn't know what she was gonna do."

"Did she tell you who the father was?"

"No, but she did say that Dusty wasn't gonna be happy."

"Who's Dusty?"

"I don't know. But whoever he was, Winter was scared of him and what he might do to her when he found out that she was pregnant."

"Thank you, Ms. Everett. You've been a big help," Carmen said, and she left The Polo Bar.

When she got back in her car, Carmen took out her phone and made a call.

"This is Detective Mitchell."

"Hey, Diane. It's Carmen."

"Hey, Carmen. What's up?"

"You got time to run a name for me?"

"What's the name?"

"It's a nickname. Dusty."

"I'll check it out and get back to you with what I find."

"Thanks, Diane," Carmen said, and she ended the call.

Carmen had been back at the station for about an hour when she got a call from Diane.

"I ran the alias 'Dusty' through the database."

"And?"

"I got a couple of possibilities, but the one that jumped out at me was Modesto Colbert, a.k.a. Dusty, a.k.a. Big Dust, a.k.a. Dusty Road."

"Why does he jump out at you?"

"His penchant for violence. He's been on and off the narcotics unit's radar for a few years. They believe that he's still in the game, just working through proxies now."

"Thanks, Diane. I'll check him out."

"No, Carmen."

"What you mean, no?"

"I mean, Colbert is a dangerous man, so no, Carmen, you are *not* going to talk to him without me."

"Okay. That works for me. I promise not to question him without you. Besides, there's somebody else I wanna talk to before I talk to him."

Chapter Thirty-four

Adam Gatewood.

One of the men who testified against Akira Dennison. Like all the rest of her prey, Gatewood had moved on and had given up the drug game for the most part. He would still stick his hand in to do a deal if there was enough money involved to make it worth his while. Now, Gatewood, like Colbert, was masquerading as a legitimate businessman. Gianna discovered that Gatewood had recently acquired a nightclub called Cloud 67.

When Gianna and Carter arrived at Cloud 67, they went to the bar.

"What can I get for you?" the bartender asked as he dropped bar napkins in front of them.

Carter looked at Gianna. "What are you drinking?"

"I'm feeling like something different. What do you recommend?"

"Jungle Bird," the bartender said. "It's a mixture of rum, Campari, pineapple juice, lime juice, and demerara syrup."

"Sounds good. I'll try that."

"And one for the gentleman?"

"No. I'll have a shot of Hennessy. Paradis, if you got it."

"I have XO."

"That will do," Carter said, and the bartender went to pour their drinks.

When he returned, he placed the cocktails in front of Carter and Gianna.

"What else can I get for you?"

Gianna put a hundred-dollar bill on the bar.

"I need a little information."

The bartender looked around, and then he quickly snatched up the money and put it in his pocket.

"What do you wanna know?"

"Adam Gatewood. He here?"

The bartender looked around and leaned forward.

"I haven't seen him tonight. He usually comes in about two or three in the morning to get the money off the bar and the door."

Gianna glanced at her Versace watch.

"Thanks," she said, and she and Carter found a table to wait for Gatewood to arrive.

"So, what's the deal with you and these two?" Carter asked.

"When Adam got arrested, they offered him immunity for his testimony, and he gave them me and Modesto. We got busted at the same time. Neither of us knew at the time that it was Adam who gave us up. He was still on the street while we were locked up. I trusted him," Gianna spat out. "Trusted him to keep the program going. Then, right before we were scheduled to go to trial, my lawyer told me that Modesto's lawyer had partitioned to separate our cases. He pleaded guilty to criminal possession in the seventh degree of a controlled substance, and the next thing I knew, he was testifying against me. What I didn't know was that Adam and Modesto had been working together against me all along. While he was locked up, Adam ran things until he got out."

"What about Colbert? What's his deal?"

"Honestly, I don't know."

"What do you mean, you don't know?"

"I mean that I have no idea where he is or how to get to him." Gianna paused. "The word I get is that something happened about a year ago, and after that, Modesto became reclusive. Dropped out of sight and was letting Winston Townson run things for him. That is, until somebody killed him."

Carter smiled to himself since he was responsible for taking Townson off the board.

"I was hoping that would bring Modesto out of his hole." Gianna shook her head. "No such luck. Some chick named Tanisha Hickman stepped into his spot."

"You ever think of using her to find Colbert?"

"I have. But I'm patient—one thing at a time. Once I get Adam, I'll turn my attention to finding Modesto," Gianna said, and Carter nodded, but patience never was his strong suit.

It was almost three in the morning when Gatewood came into Cloud 67. Gianna tapped Carter.

"There he goes," she said, and they watched him go to the office in the club.

"How do you wanna play this?" Carter asked.

"Wait until he comes out and follow him."

"Right," Carter said, but shaking his head. "I have a better idea."

"What's that?"

"We create our own opportunity. We make Gatewood tell you where Colbert is before we kill him, and then we go kill Colbert." Carter finished his drink and signaled for a server. "Let's get this over with so we can move on."

"I like the sound of that." Gianna smiled. "But tell me something."

"What's that?"

"Are we moving on together?"

"If that's what you want."

"What about you? What do *you* want?"

"I think us moving on together might be interesting."

"I think it'll be fun," Gianna said as a server arrived at their table.

"What can I get for you?"

"Jungle Bird for the lady, and I'll have a shot of Hennessy XO neat."

Thirty minutes later, Gatewood came out of the office with another man.

"We're up," Carter said, and they got up.

Carter and Gianna followed the pair out of the club and watched as the man escorted Gatewood to his car. They hurried to Carter's car so they could follow him. When they stopped at the Hotel 365 on Grand Concourse in the Bronx and went inside, Carter and Gianna followed them into the building. They watched as Gatewood went into a room while the man stood guard at the door.

"What now?" Gianna asked.

"Give me your gun."

Gianna went into her purse and took out her weapon. She handed it to Carter.

"Come on," he said and began walking down the hall.

When the man at the door looked their way, Carter raised Gianna's silencer-clad weapon and shot him. Once they got to the door, Carter shot him again.

"Check his pockets for a key," he said, and Gianna searched him.

She held up the key. "Got it," she said, and then she opened the door.

Carter dragged the body into the room, and Gianna silently closed the door behind them. He handed Gianna her gun.

"Thanks."

"You're welcome," she said, and that was when she heard it. "Sounds like somebody's getting busy in here." Gianna raised her weapon.

Carter took out his gun, and they followed the sounds of passion to the bedroom, where they found that Gatewood had a woman bent over the edge of the bed. The sound of flesh pounding against flesh and her screams allowed Gianna to walk up to him and put her gun to his head.

"Hello, Adam."

When Gatewood felt the gun against his temple, he froze.

"Why did you stop?" the woman asked, looking over her shoulder. She screamed when she saw Carter. She quickly rolled away from Gatewood and tried to cover herself.

"Get dressed and get outta here," Gianna said, and the woman hurried to dress. "Watch him," she said, and Carter put his gun to Gatewood's head.

She looked around the room until she saw his pants. She picked them up and tossed them on the floor in front of Gatewood.

"Put some pants on."

As Gatewood picked up his pants and put them on, Gianna picked up the woman's purse. She took out her driver's license.

"Joanna Cortez." She held up the license. "I'm gonna keep this in case you wanna get talkative, and I have to come visit you," Gianna said and then escorted the woman out of the room.

"What's this about?" Gatewood asked when Gianna returned to the room.

"Ask the lady. I'm just along for the ride," Carter said, and Gatewood looked at Gianna.

"What's this . . . about?" he asked slowly, and then he looked closely at her. "Akira?"

"You recognized me. I'm impressed."

"It's those eyes, Akira. I will never forget those eyes. I thought you were somewhere in South America."

"I was. And then I started thinking about you and all the people who betrayed me, so here I am."

"It was you, wasn't it? It was you who killed Allen Lee, Brandon Perez, Paul Mason, and Charley Pacheco."

"Keaton Douglas and Philip Parrish too."

"So, what now?"

"Well, Adam, it's simple; you're gonna tell me how to find Modesto."

Gatewood laughed. "Fuck that. I ain't telling you a fuckin' thing."

"Then I sincerely hope that pain is something you enjoy," Gianna said, raised her weapon, and shot Gatewood in the leg.

He grabbed his leg and cried out in pain. "Fuck!"

Carter punched him in the face, and Gatewood went down from the force of the blow.

"Watch your language in front of the lady," Carter said, and he started kicking Gatewood.

"Where's Modesto?" Gianna shouted and shot Gatewood in the other leg.

"Fuck you!" Gatewood yelled, and Carter kicked him in the mouth.

Now, Gianna shot him in the arm. "Tell me how to find Modesto, or the next shot will be to that big dick you were slinging."

Gatewood held up his hands. "Okay, okay!" he shouted, but Carter kicked him anyway. "He lives in a white house on Berkshire Road in Bethpage."

"Thank you," Gianna said, and then she shot Gatewood in the head.

Chapter Thirty-five

"Who is it?" Elizebeth McWalter asked.

"It's Carmen Taylor, Mrs. McWalter."

She opened the door. "Hello, Ms. Taylor. I wasn't expecting you."

"And I am so sorry to just drop by like this, but I have a question to ask. May I come in?"

Elizebeth McWalter stepped aside. "Please, come in."

"Thank you. And thank you for seeing me. I won't take up much of your time, I promise."

Elizebeth held up her glass. "Can I offer you something to drink?"

"Whatever you're drinking is fine," Carmen said, and she followed her into the living room.

Once she poured Carmen a glass of bourbon and she refreshed hers, Elizebeth sat across from Carmen.

"What question can I answer for you?"

"Did Patsy ever mention a man named Dusty to you?" she asked, and Elizebeth's hand shook a bit. She dropped her head, and when she looked up, she shot the rest of her drink. She looked at Carmen and stood up, went to the bar, and poured herself another shot of bourbon.

"You know, don't you? You've known all along, haven't you?"

Elizebeth nodded her head. She returned to the sofa and sat across from Carmen.

"Patsy was pregnant, and he was the father of her child, wasn't he?" Carmen said more than she asked.

"Yes." Elizebeth paused, and then she looked at Carmen.

"What can you tell me about him?"

"I only met him once, and I told Patsy that he wasn't the kind of man she should be involved with. But she always did gravitate toward that type of man."

"What type of man was he, Mrs. McWalter?"

"She wouldn't say what he was involved in, but I've seen his type before. I believe that he was a drug dealer. She didn't deny it when I asked, so I assumed I was right."

"Please, go on, Mrs. McWalter. I know it can't be easy talking about this."

Mrs. McWalter nodded solemnly, now determined to tell Carmen the truth about what happened to her daughter.

"And then she told me that she was pregnant." She shook her head. "That was totally unacceptable. I was able to convince her not to keep the baby, and I arranged for her to have an abortion."

Mrs. McWalter paused as tears rolled down her cheeks.

"Take your time, Mrs. McWalter."

"I came to check on her the next day, and that's when I found her." Her tears now cascaded down her cheeks. "She was still alive when I found her. I asked her who did it, and she said that she had told him about the abortion, and he went crazy and beat her."

"That's why you called the doctor instead of the police, right?" Carmen asked, and Mrs. McWalter nodded.

"By the time Dr. Ritchie got here and said there was nothing he could do, Fredrick was here by that time, and he didn't want to tell the police."

"Why not?"

"He said that the police would probably never find out who Dusty was, and we should think about the family name and our reputation in the community." Mrs. McWalter paused, and then she angrily repeated what her husband said to her that day. "'How would it look if some drug dealer murdered our daughter? We'd be dragging the family name and her memory through the mud.' I told him that I didn't care about any of that." Elizebeth paused to wipe away her tears. "Then he said that it wouldn't bring Patsy back to us." Mrs. McWalter looked up at Carmen. "I agreed with that. I couldn't care less about the family name and our reputation in the community. But I agreed that nothing was going to bring my baby girl back to me."

"I promise to keep it as quiet as I can."

"I don't care anymore. Screw Fredrick. He's planning a future run for Congress, and it wouldn't look good to his Republican buddies."

"We know that Dusty's real name is Modesto Colbert."

"I hope that you lock him up and throw away the key. Rot in hell, bastard."

Carmen stood up. "Thank you for seeing me, Mrs. McWalter," she said and left the house.

As soon as Carmen got into her car, she called Detective Mitchell and told her what she had learned from Elizebeth McWalter.

"You stay away from Colbert, Carmen. Let the police handle it from here."

"I won't go anywhere near him, I promise. He's all yours, Diane. My days of danger and excitement are over for sure."

"Yeah, right, Carmen. Until the next time," Detective Mitchell said and ended the call.

Chapter Thirty-six

Gianna and Carter were quiet during the hour-and-a-half drive from the Bronx to Bethpage. Although there wasn't a lot of talking going on, every once in a while, each would look over at the other and exchange knowing glances.

No words were needed.

Both Carter and Gianna allowed themselves to think beyond their immediate actions and were thinking optimistically about the potential future they could have together. Once again, his mind drifted back to the advice that Black had given him.

Find one who holds your attention, and she isn't a murderer.

Carter looked at Gianna and thought that maybe she was a murderer, but he was a murderer too. *Does that make us perfect for each other?* Carter didn't know, but he was willing to find out.

It was the same for Gianna.

She had been alone for so long. Even when she was free back in the day, she never had time for relationships. There was always money to be made and power to wield. In those days, Akira Dennison was addicted to power and money. It was her drug of choice. She couldn't remember ever feeling for a man the way she was starting to feel about Carter. *Does that mean we are meant to be together?* Gianna didn't know the answer to that question either, but, like Carter, she was willing to give it a chance. Besides, what did she have to lose? She couldn't see a downside.

Gianna glanced over at Carter. For as long as she could remember, she had been the alpha female in just about every situation she'd been a part of. Gianna appreciated that he took charge, deciding what they would do and how they would do it.

Carter Garrison had no vested interest in her quest for revenge. There was nothing in it for him or The Family that he put before all else.

At least as far as she knew.

As far as Gianna was concerned, he was doing it all for her. And that made her feel warm inside. Another feeling that she was unaccustomed to.

But I could get used to it, she thought.

As they arrived in Bethpage, Gianna paused to think that, at that moment, she was standing on the verge of being done with her need for revenge.

Maybe it is time to try something new, she thought.

Inside the house, Modesto Colbert was sitting in the living room with his two bodyguards, Gus Jenkins and Irwin Faulkner. They had just finished a dinner of chicken florentine, marsala shrimp parmigiana, and grilled salmon, which they had delivered from Italiano Ristorante. Now, they were watching reruns of *Living Single* because Modesto thought Max, who Erika Alexander played, was sexy as hell. However, Jenkins and Faulkner thought that Kim Fields, who played Regine, was the one to watch.

In the time since he beat Patsy Winter McWalter to death, Modesto Colbert had withdrawn into himself. He didn't mean to do it. He didn't intend to kill her. He had convinced himself that he could learn to love her over time. But when she told him that she had aborted the child, his child, Modesto lost control.

Now, he very rarely ever left the house, and when he did, it wasn't for long. There wasn't much he felt like doing these days. Where Modesto once enjoyed eating in the best restaurants, closing nightclubs, throwing the most extravagant parties, and experiencing the pleasures of many different women, often at the same time, none of that held any interest for him now.

Not anymore.

He had seen what that life, a life filled with drugs and violence, had earned him. He had murdered the mother of his child. Beat her to death unmercifully.

Now, he was alone.

Modesto was overjoyed when Winter told him she was pregnant with his baby. He had thoughts about them having their baby and raising their child together. Modesto thought about putting the drug game in his rearview mirror and doing something positive with his life. He was going to be a father. He had to set a good example for his child. But those good feelings were short-lived when Winter told him that she had aborted the baby.

He snapped.

Modesto didn't remember anything after that first blow. He struck her so hard that it broke her jaw. Winter's pleas for him to stop fell on deaf ears. The next thing that he remembered was standing over her beaten and bloody body. He was covered in blood, and she was barely alive.

Instantly regretting what he had done, Modesto panicked.

He rushed into the bathroom and washed off the blood. He had some clothes in Winter's apartment, so he quickly changed and packed up anything that pointed to his ever being in the apartment before he left.

In the days that followed, Modesto backed away from the drug game. He handed power to Winston Townson.

He had made plenty of money in the game over the years and had moved into legitimate businesses. Those proved to be profitable, so he didn't need money, and the chase to gain paper and power, which was the essence of the drug game, no longer seemed worth the effort. For Modesto Colbert, all there was now was his regret over what he had done to Winter.

Once he reached Berkshire Road, Carter drove slowly down the street. Gianna pointed out the white house, and he kept moving. He parked the car around the corner from the house.

"You ready to go do this?" Carter asked when he put the car in park.

"How you wanna do it?" Gianna answered his question with a question.

Carter looked at her. "I'm gonna go to the house, ring the bell, and ask for Modesto."

"Just like that?"

"Just like that."

"Then I guess I'm ready," Gianna said and got out of the car. She stood there and waited for Carter to come around.

"Let's go."

"Before we go."

Gianna put her arms around Carter's neck and kissed him. He held her tightly. When their lips parted, she stepped back.

"Let's go end this."

"After you," Carter said, extending his hand graciously.

As they got closer to the house, Carter took out his gun, so Gianna did the same. As he said he would, Carter rang the bell. He stepped aside and allowed Gianna to stand in front of the door. She put her gun behind her back and put on a big smile. Carter raised his weapon.

"You expecting somebody?" Faulkner asked.

"No. I'm not expecting anybody," Modesto said. "Go see who it is, Gus."

Jenkins stood up and went to the door. He looked out the peephole.

"Some woman," he said.

"See what she wants, then get rid of her," Modesto ordered.

When Jenkins opened the door, Carter was standing there.

"Modesto here?" Carter asked, and then he shot Jenkins in the face.

As Modesto and Faulkner went for their guns and took cover in the dining room, Carter and Gianna rushed into the house, firing shots. They took cover when Modesto and Faulkner began firing back. The four exchanged shots until Modesto bounced up suddenly and ran, firing shots as he raced out of the room.

"I'm going after Modesto," Gianna shouted.

Carter kept firing as Gianna got to her feet, fired several shots at Faulkner, and went after Modesto. When he got to the staircase, he turned quickly and started firing at Gianna before he ran up the stairs. She stopped at the bottom of the stairs and fired at him before she climbed up.

Gianna stopped at the top of the landing and looked around with her gun raised. She could see four doors, and it was apparent that one was a bathroom. Gianna knew that Modesto was in one of those rooms.

But which one?

She took a deep breath and opened the first door she got to. Gianna looked inside, and then she stepped in. She looked in the closet and under the bed before she moved into the next room. She could hear the shooting going on downstairs and hoped Carter would be all right as she reached for the doorknob. She looked inside, and then she slowly stepped in.

Modesto put the barrel of his gun to Gianna's temple and pulled the trigger. As her blood splattered against the wall, Gianna fell on the bed.

Carter heard the shot.

He stood up quickly and fired at Faulkner. He shot him in the shoulder, and he dropped his gun as he fell to the floor. Carter rushed toward the stairs and shot Faulkner twice more as he passed.

Modesto heard Carter coming up the stairs and left the room with Gianna's body lying dead on the bed. When Carter reached the top of the stairs, he raised his weapon and moved slowly down the hall. When he passed the room, Carter looked in and saw Gianna's body on the bed.

"Oh no."

He rushed into the room to get to her. He saw the blood pooling around her head. He sat down on the bed next to her and kissed her on the cheek, then closed her eyes. Meanwhile, Modesto emerged from hiding and sprinted for the stairs. When Carter heard the sound of footsteps going down the stairs, he kissed Gianna once more and then went after Modesto.

Modesto made it down the stairs and ran for the door. He opened the door and darted outside . . . and that's when the police lights hit him.

"Modesto Colbert! This is the police! Drop your weapon!"

Carter went to the window and watched as Modesto slowly laid his gun on the ground.

"Put your hands behind your head, interlock your fingers behind your head, and turn around slowly!"

He did as he was told.

"Now, walk slowly toward me!" the officer commanded.

Once the police handcuffed Modesto and took him into custody, Carter came downstairs and left the house through the back door. He made his way back to his car, thinking about what might have been.

Chapter Thirty-seven

After seeing how Honey handled hosting the last captain's meeting, Kelsey volunteered to host the next one at Knuckles's joint, and she vowed not to be outdone. Since Honey had called Cuisine and asked them to prepare their standard business meeting buffet, Kelsey knew that she had to one-up her. She called Imperial Caters, the top African American caterer in the city. Where Honey ordered the standard self-serve buffet, Kelsey had Imperial include staff to serve the food.

Rain shook her head. "Too much."

At Rain's insistence, the food wouldn't be served until after she completed her meeting. Now that her captains had arrived, Rain was about to get started when Black walked in with Michelle.

"Don't mind us," Black said as they sat down in the back of the room.

"Okay," Rain said and looked at RJ and Ryder. "New captains' report."

"We've recruited new muscle and placed them in our spots," RJ reported. "Along with the security the spots already had, we should be good."

"What about the soft targets like Cuisine and La Chat?" Rain asked.

"They have new people too," Ryder added. "I even let Mercedes approve the guys who will be working for her."

"I'm sure she appreciated that," Rain laughed.

"She pitched a bitch when I showed up with the first group of guys." Ryder posed to imitate Mercedes. *"My God, Ryder, you certainly don't expect me to allow those bums in my establishment."* Ryder laughed. "You know how she is."

"I put together what we've been calling a 'react team,'" Jackie reported. "It'll be Money, Baby Chris, Judah, Geno, Bowie, and Angel. If something jumps off at one of the spots, at the first sign of trouble, the operators know to call the react team. And I spoke to Monika. She and her team will back up the react team in case we need the heavy shit."

"Carter?" Rain said and awaited his report.

"As long as the react team and our people do what they're supposed to do, I don't see any reason that we can't keep doing business as usual," he said.

Rain nodded. "Understand this and make sure that everybody understands that, at this point, this is a totally defensive operation. We aren't trying to go to war with the Montanaris, but if they come at us, I want us to respond with superior force. That's all I got," Rain said and looked at Black. He stood up and came to the front of the room.

"It sounds like everybody is on top of this. I reached out to Angelo about arranging a sit-down with the Montanaris tomorrow night. Let's all hope that you did all that shit for nothing." Black nodded at Rain.

"That's it. Y'all can go eat now," Rain said.

Now that the meeting was over, Carter stood up, and instead of getting in line to eat, he went to the bar and sat down. The bartender poured his captain a shot of Hennessy Paradis. Carter shot that one and pointed to the glass before the bartender walked away. He refilled the glass.

"Thanks," Carter said, and he shot that drink too.

It had been three days since Gianna Mattise, a.k.a. Akira Dennison, was murdered by Modesto Colbert. And in that time, Carter felt empty. The only light in those otherwise dark days was when Carter learned that Colbert had hung himself in his cell.

It didn't take long for him to arrange, and it was certainly worth the money he paid to see Gianna's quest for revenge satisfied. As good as that knowledge felt, it was short-lived, and it wouldn't bring her back.

While the other captains filled their plates and sat down to eat and talk shit, Carter sipped his drink and wondered if his serious relationship with women would always end with him getting his insides kicked out.

Three days ago, Carter was happy. He was excited. He was hopeful about the future. Looking forward to life with Gianna. Carter had begun to think that things would turn out differently this time for him and Gianna. He believed that he could be different. But that wasn't to be. Gianna was dead.

He thought that everything with Mileena would work out, and they would be happy together. But then she left him. It was the same with Rain. Once he had gotten comfortable and accepted that he and Rain would be parents and raise their child together, she cut him off. Rain wouldn't even talk to him. So, in each case, Carter moved on. When Mileena left him, he was fuckin' Mileena's best friend, Yarrisa Dash, Perry Dukes's wife, Glenda, Fantasy, and several other women. Carter used them to mask the pain he felt. That was fine for a while, but then, Yarrisa finally developed a conscience, Glenda moved to California to practice medicine, and Fantasy went on some kind of secret mission for Wanda.

So, once again, Carter found himself alone.

And then, one night, Rain Robinson came along, and she set the pussy out for him. Carter dove in. Each one had wanted to get with the other since the first night they met, and that lust for each other grew until it exploded. But when Rain jerked him too, Carter did what he always did to mask his pain. Only this time, he vowed only to see married women to protect his heart.

"You all right, Skipper?" Kelsey asked.

Carter was so deep in his thoughts that he hadn't noticed her standing there. He looked at her. Kelsey was a beautiful woman. That night, she was wearing a black V-neck dress with a sexy slit in the front by Givenchy.

"I'm fine, Kelsey."

"You want me to fix you a plate?"

"No, thanks. I'm not hungry."

Kelsey paused before saying, "I haven't seen Gianna Mattise in a couple of days."

Carter looked at her, and then he signaled for the bartender.

"Let's just say that Gianna's need for revenge . . ." Carter paused and watched the bartender pour his drink. "There's an old proverb that says the person who pursues revenge should dig two graves."

"I understand, and I'm sorry." Kelsey started to walk away, but then she stopped abruptly. "If there's anything you need, anything at all, just know that I'm here for you, no matter what it is."

"Thank you, Kelsey. I appreciate that," Carter said, and he watched her walk away, wondering.

Did she just set it out for me?

Not only was Kelsey a beautiful woman, but she was also married.

Married women know what they want, and once they get it, they go home to their husbands.

But no, and it wasn't just because Kelsey was married to Knuckles. In the last couple of days, a few of his usual married playmates had called, wanting to get together, but Carter turned them down.

"I'm into something right now," was the excuse he offered up to them. "I'll get with you another time."

It just wasn't where his head was at.

Carter shot his drink and was about to leave when Black walked up with Michelle.

"I'm about to get outta here," Black began. "But I wanted to ask you what happened with Modesto Colbert?"

"Cops arrested him for murdering some rich, white girl, and he hung himself in his cell."

"Good," Black said, and he walked away.

"Good night, Mr. Garrison," Michelle said, and she left with her father.

Black and Michelle got in the Alfa Romeo, and she drove them home. After they talked about her observations regarding the captains' meeting, there was nothing else said between father and daughter. Michelle was worried that if she said anything else, Black would ask her if she had decided Shayla Clark's fate.

Which she hadn't.

There were times when she thought that it was unfair for Black to ask her to decide whether they should go to war because Shayla Clark killed a made man. But she understood why he did it.

This is what she wanted.

Michelle had been complaining about not growing up in what she felt was her rightful place at her father's side. Now, she was in that place, he was preparing her for the day when she would replace Rain Robinson as boss of The Family.

But still, Michelle thought.

This wouldn't be the first time she was called upon to give the order to end somebody's life. When she was carrying power for Barbara while she recovered from being shot, Michelle gave Axe the go-ahead to handle some business with extreme prejudice. At that time, Barbara informed her that she had overstepped her authority.

"When you gave the order for Axe to kill Adams without running it by me, Jackie, or Rain, you definitely overstepped."

Michelle assumed that she would be reprimanded for her actions. When she told her parents, Shy wasn't happy about it.

"Now, she's sanctioning hits," Shy said when she heard the news. "It's not that I'm not proud of you and what you're doing. I am proud of you. You're amazing. But I'm your mother, and I want to protect you, and I want the best for you."

But she didn't work for her parents; Michelle worked for Barbara. It would fall to Barbara to reprimand her for her actions. However, Barbara surprised her.

"But fuck it. I asked you to step up, and you stepped up in a big way."

So, even though this wouldn't be her first time, this was different. It wasn't just a matter of whether somebody lived or died. Michelle had to decide whether to take The Family to war. Not going to war meant that Shayla Clark had to be handed over to the Montanaris.

And they would surely kill her.

Chapter Thirty-eight

When they got to the house, Michelle said good night to her father and went upstairs to her room. She was glad that he didn't ask her about what she had decided to do.

The following morning, Black was awakened by a phone call from Roland.

"Sorry to bother you, Mr. Black, but Ms. Moore is here to see you."

"Let her in," Black said and sat up in bed.

"What's going on?" Shy asked.

"Wanda is here."

"Tell her I said hello," Shy said, fluffing her pillow. Then she rolled over and went back to sleep.

When Black got downstairs, Wanda was waiting for him in the media room.

"Hi, Mike," she said.

She was behind the bar, fixing herself an apple martini. Since James was murdered, she had been drinking more than she should, and she'd be the first one to admit it.

"Morning, Wanda."

"You want me to fix you one while I'm back here?"

Black sat down. "I need to eat something first."

"Since when?"

"I ain't as young as I used to be."

"You don't have to worry." Wanda came from behind the bar and sat down. "I stopped in the kitchen to say hello. Your mother cooked."

"Good to know." Black paused. "So, what brings you out so early this morning?"

Wanda took a sip of her martini and paused before she said, "I heard Michelle was at the captains' meeting with you last night."

"Word travels fast."

"It's the talk of The Family."

"And?"

"You're grooming her, aren't you?"

"Yes, Wanda, I am. One day, all of this might fall to her to command. And if that day comes, she *is* going to be ready."

"Until then?"

"Until then, what?"

"What is she in The Family?"

"She works for Barbara."

"Okay, Mike. Don't get excited. I was just asking a question. She is your daughter. People are going to assume that power and position go along with it."

"One." Black held up one finger. "I don't give a fuck what people think. If you or Bobby have a problem with it, I am more than ready to listen to what you have to say about it." He raised two fingers. "Two, yes, Michelle is my daughter, and to me, that means that she has to earn power and position. Not have it handed to her. We didn't hand RJ his position. No. We did everything we could to make sure that he was ready. And when his time came, he earned it. And like I said, when the time comes, Michelle *will* be ready."

"I don't have a problem with it."

"Then why are you here so early in the morning?"

Wanda smiled. "I wanted to know if you wanted me to go with you when you sit down with the Montanaris."

Black shook his head. "If you wanna go, you know you're more than welcome."

"Good, then I'm coming with you. Who are you bringing with you?"

"I was going by myself. But now that you're going, I know Bobby is gonna wanna go with us."

Excited, Wanda asked, "You want me to call him?"

"Go ahead." Black stood up. "I'll be in the kitchen."

When breakfast was ready, the family gathered at the table to eat. That morning, M prepared eggs Benedict, rolls, and steak and eggs with herb-roasted cabbage, and hash browns. Michelle was the last one to arrive at the table.

"Morning, everybody."

"Good morning," her father said as she grabbed a plate.

"Did you sleep well?" Joann asked.

"No, Grandma Jo. I had a lot on my mind, so I tossed and turned all night." Michelle sat down at the table.

"What's on your mind?" Shy asked.

Michelle glanced at Black. "I gotta make a decision," she said.

"Have you?" Black asked.

"I have."

"And?" Black inquired.

"I decided that you're right. It's more than just a simple math problem."

He nodded.

Everybody at the table looked back and forth between Black and Michelle, wondering what was going on.

"What's more than a simple math problem?" Shy asked.

"Our people. And our loyalty to them," Michelle answered, and Shy nodded.

She didn't understand what that meant. However, Shy assumed that it was something between Black and Michelle, and that was enough for her.

Later that evening, Chuck drove Black, Bobby, and Wanda to Angelo's private club in Yonkers. While Chuck waited at the bar, Joey escorted them to the office, where Angelo was waiting.

"This is a surprise," Angelo said when he saw Wanda come in with Black and Bobby. He always made a fuss over Wanda every time he saw her.

"How are you, Angelo?" She gave him a hug and a kiss on the cheek.

"Better than most. What about you?"

"I'm awesome."

Once everyone was seated, Black asked the question he had been thinking about since they set the meeting.

"What can you tell me about Salvatore Marino?"

"He's the boss of the Montanaris," Angelo began. "He became boss when Marcell De Luca died a couple of months ago. The Commission decided that Nicodemus Conti wasn't up to the task."

"Why was that?"

"The old guy's got dementia. But even though he ain't boss, he still carries weight, and he's got a lot of friends." Angelo took a sip of his drink. "I mention this because Giovanni Folliero is Conti's nephew. He's the one who is pushing this thing. Because honestly, Giovanni Folliero was a piece of shit."

Just then, there was a knock at the door. Joey stuck his head in. "The Montanaris are here, Angee."

Angelo looked at Black. "You ready, Mikey?"

"Yeah. Let's get this over with."

When Joey returned to the office with the Montanaris, Angelo, Black, Bobby, and Wanda stood up.

"Sal, how are you?" Angelo asked and shook hands with Salvatore Marino.

"I'm good, Angelo." He turned to face Black.

"Salvatore Marino, this is Mike Black, Bobby Ray, and Wanda Moore."

"It's an honor to meet you," Marino said.

Black shook his hand. “Same here.”

“My associates, Cesare Ricci and Gianpaolo Agosti,” Marino said, and everybody shook hands.

“Please, everybody, have a seat,” Angelo said, and everybody sat down.

“I want to start by saying thank you, Mr. Marino—”

“Sal.”

Black nodded. “Mike.”

Each man nodded as a show of respect.

“Thank you, Sal, for agreeing to this meeting. Hopefully, we can resolve this matter and move forward.”

Marino nodded. “As I said, Mike, it was an honor to meet and sit down with you. Angelo here tells me that you’re an honorable man, and I thought that we should say whatever we have to say to each other’s face.”

“I agree with you.”

“We’re here about the murder of Giovanni Folliero by Shayla Clark,” Marino began.

“He killed her brother. She had every right to kill him,” Black countered.

“I’m aware of the circumstances.”

“I meant no disrespect.”

“Believe me, Mike, none was taken,” Marino said with a smile. He paused and looked around the room. “You mind if you and me talk alone?”

“Not at all,” Black said. “Give us the room.”

Bobby and Wanda stood up right away, as did Angelo. Marino looked at Ricci and Agosti.

“It will be all right,” he said.

They each nodded, stood up, and left the room with the others.

“Here’s the deal, Mike,” Marino said once they were alone. “Like I said, I know all about it. And I’m gonna be honest with you. Giovanni Folliero was a piece of shit. Ain’t nobody sad to see that bastard go. But he was a made man. An honor that asshat didn't deserve. Nicodemus Conti is the prick's uncle. Him and my predecessor, Marcell De Luca, came up together."

"I understand how that goes."

"Then you understand that my hands are tied here."

"Nothing we can do to work this out peacefully?"

"Honestly, Mike, if it were entirely up to me, I'd say good riddance to that numskull and thank you for your people putting him out of everybody's misery. But it ain't entirely up to me. Like I said, the old man still carries some weight." Marino stood. "There will be no peace until Shayla Clark is dead, and you hand over her dead body."